INDIGO

MARCUS WOOLCOTT

Paperback ISBN -978-1-907690-01-3

Kinglake Fiction

With thanks to Amanda and Sonya

Here Men From The Planet Earth.
First Set Foot Upon The Moon.
July 1969 AD
We Came In Peace For All Mankind

Kira knew the words by heart now. Regardless, she read it again. Those on the ticket desk were used to her and probably smart enough to see why it was such a draw, but they said nothing.

She leant forward in the seat and looked at the moon buggy, twiddling nonchalantly with the white strip in her hair.

The Moon had become a tourist attraction just two seasons after the Earth had been destroyed. It was hardly the greatest crowd-puller, but species still came, mainly for the same reason that they would go and visit the site of a great massacre or historic blunder. The wonder of witnessing something that went badly wrong with disastrous consequences. There was a Museum of Earth, a tour, and even clothing with "Visit the moon, the view's a lot better nowadays." or "Save the galaxy, eat a human."

Kira was sat on a seat inside one of the translucent tunnels that ran around the original landing-site. She wore a hood to keep recognition down to a minimum. Occasionally she would be spotted and either get a distasteful stare or some pathetic quip, but she could handle it now. She felt at peace here. Even though - from what she had heard - she had little in common with

5

humans, it was still soothing to know that they had been here, walked where she now was. It made her that bit more complete.

Her right hand started to vibrate and she put her index finger to her ear. 'What is it?'

'Don't forget you still have to make that delivery, and can you pick me up one of those Moon Stress Balls?' Cesar asked.

'Yes and no.' She put her hand back down, wishing deep inside that she could have been there to see her race make that first step outside the atmosphere of their home planet. The entire population of the world rallied together, no matter how many paper rectangles you owned.

Before

The Lazis.

Like fire, the wheel, penicillin, the internet, the Lazis would change life on earth for the better.

In lengthy and well-funded collaborations with NASA and many leading Universities across the world, the Lazis was born. The man who had first conceived the idea and followed it through to fruition was a thirty-seven year old African-American: Professor Jacob Malcolm; himself soon to be a father and start a family in the new world. A much cleaner world.

The Lazis was a blue ball of crackling energy no larger than the average television set. It was able to sustain itself for years without need of recharging, gave off no fumes, required no chemicals and produced no waste, hazardous or otherwise. One Lazis was capable of powering a town for roughly ten years before it simply died out and needed to be replaced. Even the technology and creation of each individual Lazis was harmless, and, considering what it was capable of, cheap too.

Leading scientists, environmentalists and political leaders from around the world applauded Professor Malcolm, all fascinated by the complex equations and dynamics that had been used over the five years of hard labour eventually bearing fruit in the shape of something so profound and awesome in its scope that the world was now changed thanks to its very existence.

The test site was chosen: Cairns, Australia. The local power-station was shut down and used instead to house the Lazis. There was not a single problem. As promised, it was perfect: powering the town and requiring only a skeleton crew on a shift to keep an eye on things, but even they spent most of their time absorbed in other activities.

The power-station was opened to the public and many visited just to marvel at the beautiful blue globe of energy. Many opined that they found it calming to watch and couldn't wait to have one in their own homes. Thousands of wires and sensors ran from the base of the Lazis' box to houses, transformers and conductors all over the town.

From that moment, as the Lazis was declared an unbridled success, the entire world dreamed of a brighter future. Factories and cars would no longer need to pump out unhealthy exhaust fumes. Poor developing countries would never again suffer western wrath for the precious oil under their homes, and nuclear power could happily be abolished. In time, the world could now heal.

It was a lesson for all: an organism that wanted nothing more than to give.

Not everyone was happy.

Those standing in the shadows, who had been amassing great wealth from filth spewing factories and the death of eastern innocents saw no joy in this new technology. These people saw no reason why they should suddenly have to lose their primary income. In *their* world, the Lazis was not welcome.

Even though every man, woman and child on the planet knew what the Lazis implied and promised, money was still a far more powerful motivator. It took very little persuasion and a simple six-figure cash transfer to ensure that one of the scientists keeping an eye on the Lazis "screwed up".

Five seconds and a speedy data entry, and everything changed. The blip was so small and discreet that nobody took any notice of it, not even the daily status report found it worth noting.

The Lazis noticed it. In those few seconds as its initial programming was corrupted, it learnt a trait previously indigenous only to humans: greed.

No longer was it interested in giving, it had tasted power and it wanted more. For the first few weeks it had continued with its initial programming, holding back only a tiny amount for itself. Then, as it started to absorb a third of what it was giving out, alarm bells rang and it began to grow. Instantly, there were calls for it to be shut down; only this was not possible. A battery can not be shut down only disconnected and so, with great reluctance, it was. But the Lazis was not easily fooled and its raw hunger could not be abated. Electrons and tiny particles in the air became its next source of food and anything that wasn't nailed down began to very slowly inch towards the glowing ball as it stretched out wanting more. Human instinct then turned towards its destruction: lasers were fired into it, experimental foam was sprayed over it - it was even shot at. The Lazis absorbed all these and happily continued.

The records were checked, the blip was found and the relevant employee was fired - not that he seemed too upset.

Within a fortnight, the Lazis had grown to the size of a family car and showed no signs of stopping. The best scientific heads got together in a Top Secret meeting at The Pentagon, decreeing that the only option left was to plug it back in and try to absorb energy from it, transfer the energy back to other power stations in the hope that it would revert to "giving".

This proved to be the biggest mistake. The Lazis never again intended to *give*.

'Hurry!'

Professor Jacob Malcolm held open the security door for his wife, Joanne, and then closed it behind her. He then showed his own pass-card to the sensor setting off alarms and bringing down heavy defensive doors, while he placed the "authorised" one he had stolen from a fellow scientist back in his pocket.

The second he'd received that phone call telling him that his first "child" had been corrupted, he knew what had happened and it made him sick to the stomach. He had spent years of his life deliberately constructing the Lazis, wanting nothing more than to ensure the world would one day be beautiful and clean again for not just his child but generations beyond that. Unfortunately, even during its creation, men in suits walking around corridors with killer smiles and briefcases had frowned upon him. It chilled him to think that they cared more about money than their own survival and he was damned if his child was going to miss out on a chance to live because of some Business Degree Graduate's blind greed. Hence why he was back in the NASA Headquarters.

They walked briskly up blank corridors - that had not long ago been witness to incredible celebration. Alarms deafened in the background. His wife was right behind him cradling their daughter in her arms. They had discussed this for hours, neither had wanted to do it but they refused to let her die too.

They finally reached their destination and Jacob began typing away at the keyboard in an alcove by the two huge steel doors. He showed the stolen pass to the sensor and waited agonising seconds for it to be verified before being requested to enter more information which he quickly did as Joanne put a hand on his shoulder, helping him to relax somewhat.

The doors hissed open and they entered. The circular room was two hundred feet in diameter and over a hundred feet high. In the centre stood a brand new experimental rocket. It was silver and white and completely untested. The rocket had been built with a cryogenic freezing pod to allow scientists to send a primate beyond our solar system and explore the farthest reaches of space. But with the Lazis now the size of a small continent and growing every day, the project had been abandoned - like much else in the world.

Nothing could stop the Lazis now and the whole world was merely waiting for the end. Powerful political leaders had already disappeared to a secret bunker in the hope that there would be something left for them to rule when all this was over.

Chaos had hit the streets as mankind's primal urges were unleashed worldwide causing rioting, parties and unabated anarchy. But when all the beer had been drunk and all the shops had been looted, a serenity descended as everyone came to realise exactly what was going to happen. There followed, a mass migration as families travelled the world to be together at the final moment. Television and radio broadcast programmes about all the great achievements of man and just what Mother Earth had endured during her time. By this point, even the men in suits were humbled, realising fast that money was now no more valuable than toilet paper.

Jacob furiously threw his fingers over the two consoles in front of him as he looked at his watch. It wouldn't take those in charge very long to figure out what was going on. He had to work fast. Jacob also knew that the political leaders were not ensconced in a bunker, they had a bigger plan.

He was devastated that he would never get to see his daughter grow: her first steps, first day at school and whatever she chose to accomplish from there on. Pushing such thoughts from his mind, he finished typing, took an odd triangular key on a chain from his pocket and placed it around her neck.

'Hold on to this, Angel. And should you discover its use, I know you'll be able to use it properly.' He kissed the smooth, dark skin on his daughter's forehead and adjusted the thick blanket around her. He then turned to Joanne. 'Ready?'

She looked back at him, tears streaming down her face, and nodded then made her way to the stairs by the rocket. Jacob ran to the side-room housing the control consoles.

He watched through the window as Joanne reached the rocket and he opened it for her from the computer. He allowed a few seconds for his wife to place their daughter into the pod, as he had instructed, and say her own goodbyes.

Then, as she began to walk back, one hand across her mouth, tears still pouring down her face, Jacob closed the pod and began to type ferociously.

High up above them, the domed roof opened and the night sky revealed itself.

Jacob couldn't help but pray that just one of those tiny white pinpricks of light out there was inhabited by kind beings that would take care of his daughter.

Joanne joined him and he paused typing to wipe some tears from her face and point to a trapdoor and stairway to his left, promising he would join her in a moment.

Job finished, he heard the engines in the rocket began to tick over as the immense circuit boards computed the controls he had fed them and began to initiate his instructions. He then joined his wife, closing the thick trapdoor behind him. They both stood in the cramped space and watched small plumes of smoke start to pour out of the engines from the specially made window in the floor.

'She could wind up anywhere. What if she crashes into an asteroid?' Joanne asked, wrapping an arm tightly around his waist. 'We didn't even name her, Jacob.'

Jacob kissed the top of his wife's head. 'Naming her would have made it even harder to let go, and while I can't guarantee that she'll survive, she at least has a chance now.'

'I love you.'

Jacob smiled, although he had always had trouble with the "L" word, he knew she knew the feeling was mutual. 'We would have been good parents.'

'We are good parents.' His wife rested her head against his shoulder as the engines above them roared, making the entire room vibrate and then they saw nothing but flame for a few minutes.

When the flame subsided, they could both see the burning engines through the roof, high up in the sky, hopefully carrying their daughter to safety.

The next sound was machine-gun fire followed by shouting, the trapdoor was opened and they were both roughly dragged out by armed guards.

Jacob and his wife were on their knees on the control room floor, hands cuffed behind their backs. Six armed guards buzzed around the main room joined by a scientist. Another scientist was looking at the information from the consoles, while a middle-aged man in a suit and tie stood with his back to the computers, arms folded, looking down at Jacob.

Jacob knew him well: Grant Allen. The two of them had been friends at one time and it had been Grant that had helped to ensure continued funding from most of the Universities. All friendships were now forgotten thanks to Jacob's recent actions.

'That was foolish Jacob, very foolish.' He turned to the scientist. 'Is it still in range?'

The scientist nodded.

'Disable the engines and bring it back, initiate the emergency over-ride.'

The scientist tried to obey only to fail. 'The system password's been changed. I can't access it.'

Grant turned back to Jacob. 'What is it?'

Jacob scoffed. 'Forget it!'

A guard appeared at the door to confirm that the key was nowhere to be found. Grant nodded, unsurprised, and then held out his hand for a gun before turning back to Jacob and pointing the gun at Joanne. 'Don't be foolish, Jacob?'

Even though there was a brief flicker of panic in his wife's eyes, Jacob started to laugh softly. 'In another six months the Lazis will have grown so large that the Earth will be swallowed up like a gobstopper. The sun will absorb the Lazis and no trace of humanity will remain. Shooting us will make no difference.'

Grant knew he was right. Even now, a third of the world was uninhabitable desert; the Lazis was a giant wart on the side of the planet. He placed the gun down on the console. 'The President will not be happy.'

Jacob continued to laugh. 'Why should that upset me?'

Grant's expression turned into a sneer. 'This is your God-damn fault! You should have built some sort of fail-safe into it.'

'There was no need!' Jacob retaliated. 'If it hadn't been screwed with by some money-grabbing punk, it would still be running successfully to this day. The Lazis was perfect, humanity was the problem!'

At that Grant smiled briefly before sighing, and then pausing as an idea ran through his mind. He looked down at Jacob and his wife with a degree of smugness. 'Last chance Jacob, what's the password?'

Jacob remained defiant. 'Not a chance.'

Grant shrugged innocently, as if all further actions were out of his hands, then spoke to the scientist again, ensuring the two of them could hear.

'How is Project Domino?' he asked, noting Jacob's sudden attentiveness.

The scientist quickly bought the information up on the computer. 'Progressing ahead of schedule.'

'Excellent, add some new initiatives to her protocol, namely the retrieval of the key.'

'No!' Jacob strained at his handcuffs.

His wife, unaware of what "Project Domino" was, could only watch the two men as if she were watching a game of tennis.

'The password?' Grant asked once more.

Before Jacob could answer, the scientist interrupted.

'I'm sorry Sir, but the rocket is now too far out of range. It's on its own...but all systems are working perfectly, the cryogenics have already been engaged and life signs are normal.'

Grant ignored him and left the room, missing Jacob's triumphant smile and pausing only to tell a guard to release them.

Six months later, as predicted, Earth was destroyed. Absorbed by the Lazis. Still hungry, the Lazis searched for the next source of energy and quickly found it: the Sun. Mercury and Venus were in a far orbit out of reach and so the Lazis began to drift out of its home orbit. Yet, the sun, without the slightest of effort, "swallowed" the Lazis and returned to watch over its remaining eight planets as though nothing had happened. The only remnant of humanity was The Moon, now drifting all alone like a child abandoned on the steps of an orphanage.

The Draven Galaxy
Three hundred light years from Earth

The small pod drifted harmlessly through space, its one tiny occupant still in a deep dreamless sleep, unaware of the heavily-armed ship that was fast approaching. The ship was further identifiable to nearby systems by the huge dark red lettering on the side: The Genesis. The entire hull was a mass of blast craters, charred metal, or varying weapons and other odd metallic constructions, many of which looked as if they had been removed without choice from other ships and welded roughly to the side.

The pod did not go unnoticed.

Two lethal claws protruded on thick cables from the hull aiming for the pod, talons outstretched. But with only inches to spare, the entire ship was shaken by a hostile blast of energy from a nearby planet and the pod was ignored as the crew, clearly more interested in preserving their pride than picking up junk, turned their attention to the location of the blast, allowing the tiny pod to continue.

Skelia was a small planet with two tiny moons, both uninhabited. Skelia's surface was a mass of low mountain ranges with deep, vast caves within them. The mountains were surrounded by acres of dusty blue vegetation and pools of thick silvery-grey liquid known as Poole: a valued commodity in the Draven Galaxy. Every ship whether hostile or otherwise relied on it as an essential. Poole was added to engines and other machinery to ensure not only excellent lubrication between moving parts but also prevention against over-heating, and Skelia is the only place it can be found.

However, unlike the two moons, Skelia was not uninhabited, it was home to skelms. Skelms are around eight foot long and slug-like in appearance. But they do have a backbone and two forearms so spend most of their waking time upright, slithering along on their tails. They are all a deep purple in colour and have a natural plate of grey armour that runs from their foreheads to the tips of their tails. The males are slightly smaller than the females and have a dark green stripe along their sides while the larger females have a bold yellow stripe.

The skelms had been farming Poole, as they did most days, when they heard a cry from those not currently farming, and looked up to see something burning through the clouds high above them. They all watched intrigued as the object hurtled downwards at an angle, hit one of the pools, skimmed across the surface and continued across the blue tundra, digging a shallow trench as it slowed and then halted, smoke pouring from it.

While the others watched, two male skelms cautiously slithered over and peered down into the trench to see the strange metal pod before beckoning the others over. Of course, word quickly spread and by the time the pod had cooled enough to touch, there were over twenty skelms surrounding it.

One of the males that had initially investigated the pod now pressed his hand to it and then quickly drew it back as data began to rain down a small screen embedded on the surface. There was then a loud hiss and the front half of the pod shifted slightly as cool air was released and the pod began to hum.

The assembled skelms all watched, fascinated as the pod continued to hum and then water began to trickle from drainage points around the outside.

The outlet ended and there was a few minutes of silence before a shrill cry came from inside which began to grow louder.

A nearby skelm carefully pulled back the front of the pod to reveal its cargo, immediately eliciting a gasp from all around as the tiny infant appeared, crying and wailing.

A female skelm pushed past the two males and was about to pick up the infant when she was stopped.

'Don't touch it.'

'Why ever not?'

'It's a human.'

Word travelled around galaxies surprisingly quickly, especially when it regarded a race that had destroyed their own planet.

The male looked around at the others. 'I say we destroy it now.'

A few agreed but the female didn't. 'It's far too small to be any trouble; you can't kill an innocent creature.'

The crowd was now split fifty-fifty. The infant had ceased crying and was now looking around in wonder while blowing saliva bubbles.

'So what do you suggest? Keeping it? It's alright now, but these things grow. In ten-fifteen seasons it'll be a different story.'

'Not if we raise it as a skelm. With no interference from humans, it won't grow to be like them.'

This changed the local opinion to seventy-five percent in favour of letting it live.

But the male wasn't finished yet. 'We could send it back out there; let someone else worry about it?'

That didn't go down at all well, and prompted another female to raise her voice. 'You know The Genesis is in a nearby orbit, that's unthinkable.'

Finally relenting, the male sighed. 'Well, I'm not keeping it.'

The female now pushed past him and reached into the pod to remove the infant and cradle it in her arms, briefly fingering the key around her neck with interest. 'I'll look after it. We're expecting a child of our own soon. The egg should hatch any day and the two of them can be raised together.'

Another male then looked at the pod. 'NASA? Is that its name?'

The female shook her head then stuck out her slick translucent tongue and licked from the infant's stomach to her nose. 'Tastes female, and NASA is not a very feminine name. I shall call her Kira.'

Kira said nothing; she simply stretched out and made herself comfortable against the warm rubbery skin of her new mother.

21

Skelia had not been created with human beings in mind.

The skelms all lived in the caves deep inside the mountains as the year was split into two. For four months of each year, the planet was beset by terrifying storms which ravaged the surface and made leaving the cave impossible. It was only during the remaining six months that the surface was inhabitable and this time was spent harvesting poole.

Kira's 'brother Cadbur had little problem staying inside for four months, eating and doing nothing, but the minute Kira was able to walk, before she could even talk, the storms fascinated her and she would sneak out to the edge of the caves to watch them.

Diet was yet another issue.

Inside the caves grew two types of fungus: one was pale yellow, spongy and highly fluorescent. It grew on the walls and lit up the caves, giving them light. The other was black and flaky, growing in recesses, away from the light. Deep sections of the caves had all yellow fungus removed in order to grow the black fungus as this was the skelms one and only diet.

Upon feeding the black fungus to Kira she had been seriously ill and vomited for the best part of a day. This was in addition to the fact that she had no clothing other than her foundling blanket. It was of no bother for the skelms to wander as they had been born; their bodies retained fat and kept them warm. Kira had almost died of cold in the first few weeks.

Fortunately, the skelms had many favours owed them. Having no use for poole or credits, they were happy to give away the poole as and when requested. They had to ration in it order to maintain production but otherwise it was free to all. This bought them many favours and with Kira's arrival they decided to call some in.

They made a list including food and re-hydration pills; clothing and some basic toys then waited for the next poole pick-up and handed the list over. The driver enquired as to why but they fobbed him off knowing it was best not to let on that they had a human with them.

One day when Kira was four and the storm season was in full flow, she had once again wandered out to the edge of the cave to sit transfixed watching the red streaks of lightning attacking the ground or blasting the grey pools sending scarlet crackles across the surface.

As she watched, she absent-mindedly played with the key around her neck, fiddling with it. Her mother had removed it when she was a baby. She'd recently given it back to her saying that it was found in the egg with her but they didn't know what it was.

She was usually left alone when she watched the storms, however this time her mother decided to join her.

Kira rested against the warm purple flesh of her mother. 'Why am I diff'ent?' she asked. 'Why you purple and I'm brown like the caves?'

Her mother placed an arm around her shoulder. 'That's life Kira, everyone is different in some way but we all come from the same place. You came out of an egg just like everybody else.'

'I did?'

'Yes.'

Kira thought for a minute. 'I don't unnerstand. If we all come from eggs, why am I diff'ent?'

'Because you're special Kira, but inside we're all the same. Stand up.'

Kira stood up and her mother pulled her close to her stomach. 'Can you hear that?'

Kira could hear three separate sounds like someone gently clapping. 'What's it?'

'That's my hearts.' She took Kira's hand and placed it against her own stomach. 'Now what do you feel?'

Kira waited then shook her head. 'Nothing?'

Her mother placed her own hand on Kira's stomach then, puzzled, moved it higher. 'There we go.' She placed Kira's hand on her chest.' 'Do you feel that?'

Kira could feel a soft *thump-thump-thump* and smiled. 'That my hearts?'

Her mother was just about to answer when she decided that this conversation could go on for a very long time if she wasn't careful so she changed her mind.

'One day Kira, you're going to be bigger, much bigger, and when that day comes you'll be able to do anything you want.'

Kira listened, one hand still on her chest.

'Remember a little while ago when you asked me about those tiny lights in the sky and I told you they were stars?

24

Well each star has different types of beings on it. Beings of all shapes and size.'

'Can I go see?'

Her mother, like all skelms, had always been perfectly happy on Skelia, never having any interest in visiting other planets or systems, but she knew Kira wasn't a skelm and one day she would have no choice but to let her go.

'Yes, you can go and visit them.'

Kira looked up excited. 'Is there a Kira star with lot of Kiras?'

Her mother shook her head. 'No Kira and that's why you're so special. You're the only Kira.'

Kira contemplated this with a lot of thought and then agreed. 'I mus be super-special.'

'Yes Kira, you most definitely are.'

Kira wrapped her arms as far around her mother as she could and held tight. 'Love you, mum.'

Her mother held her close. 'I love you too Kira.'

Three months later the storm season was over and it was time to begin harvesting poole for the scheduled pick-ups due any day now.

While skelms hauled buckets of poole and emptied them into large vats, Kira, Cadbur and two other young female skelms ran and slithered around them playing with a large green ball. The ball was light but had a weight inside that was off centre so every time it was thrown, nobody could guess where it was going.

Kira looked up to see the ball coming towards her and took a couple of steps back. Suddenly it changed direction and fell to her left. Kira followed it not looking where she was going and fell into one of the pools. Fortunately, poole was completely non-toxic, although eating it wasn't advised, and the pool itself was shallow.

By the time Kira had hauled herself out of it, still laughing although now covered from head to toe in the thick grey liquid, Cadbur and the other two skelms had vanished. She looked around to see that the other skelms were slithering quickly back to the caves leaving the vats and buckets behind. She could see her mother calling to her, but couldn't hear anything due to the poole in her ears. She waved and then turned her head to one side and tried to scoop it out.

Kira suddenly stopped what she was doing and looked straight ahead as a ship hovered over the ground three or four pools away and then landed.

Kira instantly knew it wasn't a pick-up. This ship had weaponry on its hull and wording across the side in bold-red lettering.

The Genesis.

"Kira!" her mother called once more but Kira picked up the ball and held it to her chest as the ship's rear door opened and its crew disembarked.

The Genesis was no pick-up ship, neither was it a tourist ship or even a freight ship. The Genesis was a pirate ship, *the* pirate ship.

The Captain: Annex, strolled down the ramp amidst his crew and headed straight over to a small group of male skelms ready to meet him.

Annex was quite a sight. Easily reaching eight feet in height and just as broad. Annex's very presence was enough to strike fear into most. His thick dark-green boots were no doubt made with the skin of some poor creature that had crossed him, along with his muddy-yellow jacket. He wore dark blue baggy trousers with a large tear in one knee and no shirt. The only thing adorning his muscular chest were two thick chains that crossed and then vanished behind his back, both glowing with a soft green, throbbing light. His mouth stretched right around the sides of his face and inside were two rows of razor sharp teeth. He had no lips and his skin was thin and translucent, meaning his teeth, when his mouth was closed, looked like part of his face and gave him a terrifying visage. He had six eyes that spread in a neat row across the front of his face, and nothing atop his head.

While his crew began to pick up buckets of poole and take them back to the ship, Annex spoke to the skelms. From where Kira was she couldn't hear anything but Annex had two other creatures with him.

The creature to his left was Tushk, a female dreai. She was covered in thick black fur and was permanently labouring at a small computer console attached to her arm.

Annex was not just a pirate; he was also a keen scientist. Admittedly he had never studied medicine or

27

anatomy in any academy but that hadn't stopped him experimenting.

By his side sat one of his most successful experiments: Damocles. Damocles was no longer a recognised specie; instead he was a mixture. He had possibly ten or more legs and appendages. A variety of pincers, arms, claws and talons removed from creature's unfortunate enough to have upset Annex. In the centre of these rose a single tentacle with a large white eye that looked around frantically as Annex spoke.

It was Damocles that first noticed Kira, the huge white eye fixing on her as the tentacle bent to one side, intrigued, before blinking. Immediately he started tapping his claws on the ground, trying to get Annex's attention, whom at first just waved him away but then relented and looked down at him and followed his gaze.

All this time, Kira had not moved. She was still half drenched in poole, standing in the centre, the poole up to her waist while she held the ball tightly to her chest.

As Annex, Tushk and Damocles slowly began to wander towards her all the skelms froze, watching, while Annex's crew continued hauling poole, only pausing to glance at Kira. Not one wore a smile or a friendly greeting; they all looked at her as if her very presence was polluting the poole.

Annex stopped at the side of the pool and spoke to Tushk as Damocles watched Kira frantically, clearly itching to play with her.

'That what I think it is? Thought they were all dead?'

Tushk looked at Kira but Kira could see nothing except thick fur which moved when she spoke.

'I do believe you are correct Captain, their planet was unquestionably eradicated.' Tushk was remarkably well spoken. She lifted the computer so it was level with Kira's head and there was a brief flash of blue light.

As Tushk and Annex looked at the screen, Damocles reached towards Kira with a pincer only to find one of Annex's claws wrap tightly around his tentacle just below the eye making it bulge. Damocles pulled back his pincer and his tentacle was released.

'No question Captain, it is a human.'

'Fascinating!' Annex crouched down and beckoned Kira to come towards him.

She did as asked, still holding the ball but more for protection now.

Annex gently wiped some of the poole from her face. 'Always thought they were paler than this?'

'No Captain,' Tushk corrected him, 'they actually come in a variety of colours.'

'Wonder what they look like on the inside?'

At this Damocles started to get excited but was held back with one brief glance from Annex.

'What's your name human?' Annex spoke directly to Kira.

'My...my name Kira and I'm a skelm. I came from a egg too'

'Course you did, Kira.' Annex now grabbed a handful of her hair, immediately making her cry and begin to struggle. He bought her right up close to him until she could see nothing but his face. 'Tell me Kira, do you have a soul? He jabbed a finger in her stomach making her wince. 'Wonder where it is? I have a soul Kira, did you know that?'

Kira wasn't listening she was sobbing and crying, her eyes closed. The ball now lay by Damocles who was more interested in Kira.

'Not many species have souls, but I have one,' Annex continued, 'you want to see my soul Kira?'

Kira opened her eyes, blinking to see through the tears. Before she could speak her attention was diverted to the two green chains across Annex's bare chest which now throbbed and convulsed quickly.

Annex opened his mouth to say something but stopped when an empty poole bucket collided with the side of his head almost knocking him backwards. Immediately he released Kira and pushed her back into the pool where she fell backwards. He then stood and looked around with a brimstone stare.

Cadbur was standing on the other side of the pool waving his fist at Annex. 'Leave my sister alone, I've got plenty more buckets here!'

Annex said nothing but the chains were now writhing frantically at his chest, suddenly growing so tight he could barely stand and then easing in rapid succession, but Annex ignored them and headed for Cadbur.

'Get off my planet or I'll tell The Contra,' Cadbur shouted again as he picked up a bucket and began swinging it.

At that a few spare crew members who had decided to stand and watch burst into laughter. Even Annex smiled, if only briefly.

'Need to learn some respect,' Annex said softly before kicking Cadbur hard in the stomach making him double up and fight for breath. He then rammed a fist down on the back of his head. 'Filthy skelm, if it wasn't for the poole, this waste of an orbit you call a planet would have been wiped out.

Cadbur was in great pain but still managed to look up at Annex. 'At least we still have a planet…'

Annex didn't reply, didn't bother with a witty line or comeback, instead he cried out and fell to his knees as the chains went slack and a giant green bird-like form appeared behind him. A mass of pure energy. And like a bird it rose into the air, its eyes red with madness, and glared down at Cadbur.

There had never been any question that Annex was a thief and a pirate, never. He had sold his very planet in a gambling game and it was now a deserted rock having been mined of not just minerals and supplies but life too. However, he didn't just limit himself to stealing valuables and equipment. He had stolen a soul.

The planet Persiona was home to a race of peaceful and spiritual creatures dedicated to the belief that when their time was ready they would receive a soul of their own. Fascinated by this prospect, Annex had paid them a visit to see if he could get one for himself. When he discovered that it took many decades of quiet mediation and solitude, he changed his mind, went straight to the High Priest and murdered him.

In truth, when Annex had enquired about the soul, he had been playing. His over-confidence had become assured during his rein as Draven Galaxy's Mr. Unpopular. He wasn't welcome anywhere and he wouldn't have it any other way.

The chains were his own invention and they did the job perfectly. Very few species were able to physically see souls; Annex was one of them.

When the High Priest died, his beautiful golden soul automatically tried to return to the far stars from where it had come, but Annex had stopped it by activating a mechanism on the chains and drawing it into himself. The next hour had seen a tremendous fight as the soul struggled to free itself, furious at the fact that an ancient balance and practice had been desecrated. Annex had been thrown around the room and almost killed, but he held on and gained control.

Insane with anger and rage the soul lost its wondrous golden aura and turned an ugly green with evil and wrath. Its eyes, once only able to see beauty and splendour became a dark red. Now everyone could see this particular soul if so unfortunate enough.

That final act of evil had garnered Annex with absolute terror and respect wherever he went. Not one specie dared oppose him and if they did...

The red eyes bore into Cadbur and then with a shriek of unabated fury the soul attacked.

Nobody looked, everyone had heard the stories and they had no desire to confirm anything. The cries from Cadbur and the insane screams from the soul were enough to paint a vivid picture in their minds. Before too long Cadbur's pitiful cries ended, replaced only by a horrible "wet" thrashing sound that made even Annex's crew turn away with hands over mouths.

There was a cry from Annex of exhaustion and then the soul vanished and he fell back breathing sharply as two of his crew rushed to him and helped him to his feet.

The chains now glowed softly. Annex looked down at the unrecognisable remains of Cadbur with a horrible smile of satisfaction across his face. He then stood up and turned back to Kira.

Kira wasn't crying, she couldn't. She was mesmerized, unable to close her mouth or her eyes as she stared at what remained of her brother while the last few minutes played over and over in her mind.

Annex said nothing and began to make his way back to the ship, Tushk now at his side, completely ignoring all the skelms.

Damocles paused only to ram a sharp claw through the ball, puncturing it, before obediently following.

Once they were all inside the ship they wasted no time with goodbyes or farewells and departed, leaving Skelia with an indescribable silence.

Kira did not sleep that night. Whenever she closed her eyes she saw Annex's mad, green soul murdering her brother. She could still hear his pleading cries and clamped her hands over her ears to try and block them out. It was impossible, and when she opened her eyes all she could see in her mind was Annex's face and his voice repeating over and over.

'Do you have a soul? Do you have a soul?'

Kira didn't know if she had a soul but she hoped not. The thought of one of those green birds inside her was terrifying and made her hide under the covers.

Her mother and father had already spent the rest of the day comforting her and promised that by the time the harvest season was over there would be a new egg and a new brother for her, but this had just made her feel worse. She didn't want another brother, she wanted Cadbur back. They had also tried to explain that Cadbur's body wouldn't go to waste, his remains would be shovelled into one of the pools and then by the time the next harvest was upon them he would be helping lots of ships to run smoothly. All this achieved was a loud scream from Kira, a sprint to her bed and a dive under the covers, where she remained.

Now, stood at the entrance to their cave watching night fall over the marshland, her mother and father spoke.

'It was a shame about Cadbur; we'll start work on a new egg tomorrow,' her father said.

'Good idea,' her mother replied. 'But what was wrong with Kira? She went crazy when I tried to explain things to her and I haven't seen her since.'

'You forget one important thing dear, Kira is not a skelm, she's a human. Humans grow far more attached to things than we do.'

'I can't imagine having such powerful emotions inside of me, maybe that assisted in the destruction of their home.'

'Humans were renowned for their emotional capability, many became so consumed by them that they celebrated them in the form of "art".'

'Celebrating emotions? Whatever next.' Her mother was about to turn and go back into the cave when she stopped. 'How come you suddenly know so much about humans?'

Her father shrugged. 'I got a book from one of the pick-up drivers, figured it would come in handy, what was it called…? Ah, yes: "The weird and wonderful world of human beings". Absolutely fascinating. Did you know that if one of their kind dies they have a huge ceremony and bury the body in the ground?'

'What for?'

'That's nothing, when they create other human beings they actually engage in long and exhausting bodily contact…and *fluid transfer!*'

Her mother put a hand over her mouth, half in disbelief and half in amusement. 'I only hope Kira leaves home before she tries anything like that.'

Her father waved the suggestion away. 'I wouldn't worry. As far as we know she may be the only human left.'

Life changed.

As promised, her parents did indeed produce another egg, and a new son was born to them: Forber.

But Kira didn't want to know him.

He wasn't upset by this, neither did they fight or dislike each other, there was just nothing between them. Forber was perfectly content to amuse himself with other skelms.

Kira spent most of her time in silence. Sometimes she would wander around the marshes in solitude, head down. Other times she would sit by a pool for hours, gazing into it, oblivious to the surrounding world. And if ever there was a perfectly clear night, she could be found lying outside the cave looking up at the stars and the tiny passing ships, hypnotised.

Her parents quickly realised that although she would still join in with activities and chores if requested, she did it merely to obey and found no enthusiasm in it at all. For the next few seasons, Kira found little enjoyment or comfort in anything but solitude.

36

However, although to the skelms, Kira seemed downcast and morose, inside she was a raging hurricane of energy, desperate to leave Skelia and find more like her. She had overcome Cadbur's death to the point that she could now sleep, but the memories were still there and whenever she tried to discuss it, she was just told it was all over and there was nothing to worry about, which only served to fuel her frustration. She wanted to tell them how she felt, there were so many thoughts and questions whirring around in her mind now that she spent most of the time trying to work them out herself with the limited knowledge of life that she had - and one thing she did know was that she was alone. Admittedly, she wasn't technically alone at all; it was inside, deep within her that she felt so cut off and apart. She hated to admit it but she felt that she didn't belong here with the skelms, that maybe she had been born here by accident.

While sitting by one of the pools, she would often remove the key from around her neck and finger it, examine it. She knew every tiny indentation and groove in it to perfection now. It felt like the only clue she had as to where she belonged.

Pick-up ships also produced an effect in her now. Whenever she heard a ship approach, even though she knew most of them well, she would quickly walk back to the cave, head down, and sit in a corner quietly until they had left.

So a few seasons later when an exhausted-looking old ship arrived, she gave it no further attention and wandered back to the cave to wait for it to depart.

But it didn't leave and she felt her muscles tighten.

Often, she had timed how long it took a ship to collect the poole and leave, and she was always close.

This ship remained.

Fearing the worst, she was about to run deeper into the caves where no natural light could penetrate, when her mother appeared at the entrance to the cave.

'It's alright Kira, they're romers. Go take a look.' She then began to gather some black mushrooms from the corner of the cave.

Still unsure, Kira stood up and peered around the side of the cave entrance. The first thing she noticed was how oblivious all the other skelms were to the large ship parked on the marshland. They continued to collect poole as if the ship wasn't even there.

The ship itself was odd. There were no weapons on it at all and it was decorated in a variety of colours. The side doors were open and the gangplanks down, but she couldn't see anyone.

Then she saw them.

There were two of them, far to her right collecting poole. They weren't skelms.

They wore clothing like her and had arms and legs too. For a second Kira's heart leapt. Although the two of them had their backs to her they also had hair. One had long straight hair that was bright orange and the other had black hair that was short and scruffy. They were both dressed shabbily in a variety of old materials and clothing; all roughly stitched and yet perfectly fitted.

Before she knew it, Kira was out of the cave and wandering across the marshland to investigate.

As she grew closer, they both saw her and stood up.

They weren't "Kira's".

Their skin was similar in texture to Kira's but it was a dusky turquoise colour and they each had only three fingers per hand. However, like her they did have the same facial features and they both smiled warmly when they saw her.

The male put down his bucket. He was just less than six foot and the other, the female, was about a foot shorter.

'Hi there.' He offered Kira his hand and she shook it.

'My name's Kira.'

'Nice name,' the girl said. 'I'm Syjet and this is my brother Spawne. What are you doing here?'

Kira gave them a confused look. 'I live here…'

Now it was their turn to look confused before they both gave a collective *'Ah…!'*

Spawne picked his bucket back up. 'Why don't you come back to our ship, Kira?' He gestured towards it. 'Dad would love to meet you.'

Kira nodded and followed them back across the marshland.

The inside of their ship was amazing and Kira stopped inside the entrance and stood trying to take it all in.

The skelms had never been big on possessions, preferring to keep only what they actually needed.

Romers were vastly different and their ship was filled from top to bottom, each and every possible inch with... stuff.

Spawne and Syjet made their way through the heaps with practised ease as Kira continued to stand and stare unable to recognise a single thing. A million things from a million stars.

'Kira?' Spawne called out.

'Think we've lost her?' Syjet replied jokingly.

Kira made her way through the vast hold; trying to remember the route the others had taken while still occasionally stopping to admire something.

There was a heap of clear cubes, about two feet in diameter, each filled with a strange shadow-like substance that seemed to monitor Kira as she passed.

Hanging with thick cables from the roof, amongst other things, was a long thick black bag that every so often twitched or shuddered making Kira hurry along.

There were also heaps and more heaps upon those heaps of machinery and even an open crate containing both yellow and black mushrooms from Skelia tucked away.

She finally came to a doorway with a smiling mouth unprofessionally drawn around the frame and passed through to find cramped living quarters and further up ahead, the cockpit.

Spawne was sitting in an armchair, fixated on a small slab of rock, a heap of which was down by the side of the chair.

Syjet was standing in the doorway to the cockpit with one of the empty buckets swinging in her hand. When she saw Kira approach she motioned for her to come over.

Kira went in to see another romer who she presumed was their dad on his hands and knees beneath the main control panel. From what she could see he looked the same as them except he had stunningly white hair that flowed around his head and ended perfectly at his shoulders.

'We have a visitor, Father,' Syjet said.

'We do? Okay, hold on…and take this.' He handed her another empty bucket before crawling backward on his hands and knees, brushing himself off and then standing to face Kira.

His long white hair was no indication of his age at all and, although he had a few epoch lines on his face, his eyes were young and full of life.

'Hello…,' he paused and "scanned" Kira with interest. 'My name's Dylore.'

'Kira.'

She smiled at him and yet he continued to look at her as if trying to see right through her. There was fascination in his eyes. 'Mm, you must be about ten now?'

Kira shrugged and then looked around. 'Where's your wife?' she asked.

Syjet's face changed slightly and Dylore rested a hand on her shoulder.

'We were attacked by pirates and she was unfortunate…' Dylore tried to sugar coat it.

Kira nodded in understanding. 'My brother was killed by Annex, but that was ages ago now and I'm over it, we've had a new brother called Forber and although we do get on it's not quite the same as it was between me and Cadbur. Cadbur was great, he tried to protect me against Annex but Annex killed him with his green soul bird and it had red eyes and Cadbur was just trying to protect me and he killed him-'

Kira stopped as Dylore rested a hand on her shoulder making her jump. She suddenly realised there were tears pouring down her cheeks and her muscles were taught.

Dylore knelt down in front of her. 'skelms aren't very good at crying are they?'

Kira shook her head as another tear rolled down her cheek.

Soon the four of them were sat in the living quarters as Kira told them everything, finally able to release everything she had been holding in, filling them in with every tiny detail and opinion that she had pondered since Cadbur's death. And they all listened with interest, never interrupting her except maybe to ask a question or get her to elaborate on something, and as it went on Kira began to feel herself relaxing, not just her body but deep within herself. It felt wonderful; she felt like there was light awakening deep inside her, pushing away all the dark clouds that had formed.

Then, it was her turn to curl up on the seat and listen to them telling her all about their wife and mother. The happy memories they had shared as a travelling family and just what had happened the day the pirates had attacked.

Dylore related the story - with the odd addition from Spawne that he had forgotten, while Syjet sat with her knees up against her chest, occasionally sniffling as the memory was rejuvenated.

When they had finished and silence settled over them all Spawne stood up clapped his hands. 'But hey, life goes on.'

None of them could quite place what it was about the sentence that was so funny, or whether it wasn't funny but just a matter of good timing. Nonetheless they all three burst into laughter. It was a beautiful bitter-sweet shower of good emotions. The perfect crescendo now that their minds had been purged of all negativity and sadness leaving room in their hearts for the good memories to return and take pride of place.

By the time they had all finished, Dylore looked out of the cockpit window to see that it was quickly growing dark and the suns were beginning to set.

'You best head back home now Kira, before it gets dark.'

'Yeah…' Kira noticed the reluctance in her voice and the silent sigh that followed. 'Will you still be here tomorrow?'

Spawne nodded, 'sure will, got a few things to tinker with. We plan on being here until the next season begins. We'll also help the skelms with their harvest; earn some extra poole before we go.'

'Great.'

Knowing that, Kira was only too happy to leave them, waving as she ran back over the marshland to her cave. That night she slept the most peaceful and fulfilling sleep that she could remember. She slept so deeply and for so long that by the time she finally awoke the next day the cave was empty as everyone had already gone to help with the harvest. Kira stretched out, feeling like a new person, unable to wipe the smile from her face.

True to their word, the romers stayed and Kira had never noticed the days pass so fast. Some days, the four of them would just walk over the marshes, far beyond the caves and then set up a camp site and stay up late as they talked. Other times, Dylore would show her around the hold, introducing her to artefacts and items from across the Draven Galaxy. Some things were almost beyond her levels of comprehension and made her head swirl but when Dylore played her some "music"; Kira was hypnotised and listened intently. Having never heard anything like it before, she could only stand enraptured by the wondrous sounds coming from the small box in his hands as he watched her reactions with interest.

It finished and Dylore watched as Kira remained still mesmerised by the sounds.

'I take it you've never heard anything like that before?'

Kira could only shake her head. 'It's beautiful, makes me want to cry and then burst into laughter, but the skelms don't understand me when I do.'

Dylore nodded in understanding and then vanished into a heap, searching. Finally he pulled out a small red box and handed it to her.

'I wouldn't normally give something like this to someone so young, but you're going to need it. As you get older and travel you'll find less and less races will understand you and this will help you blend in a bit better.

She opened the box to see a strange black rectangular device, small enough to fit comfortably in her hand. On one side was a trigger and on the other side a silver nozzle with about ten tiny spikes. There was also a small pile of loose transparent capsules in the box, each containing a murky-orange liquid.

As she examined one, Dylore put the music back on, reverting her attention so successfully that she didn't notice him take the device and load one of the capsules into it. It wasn't till he pressed it to her upper arm and pulled the trigger that she jumped and stopped listening to the music.

'Ouch.' She rubbed her arm.

'So what do you think of the music now?'

Kira shrugged her shoulders. 'It's...I don't feel anything!'

Dylore held a capsule up to the light. 'It's called zeme. A wondrous little drug that nullifies all emotions instantly. Picked it up on Alphad; no idea where they got it mind. It's yours if you want it and I should have some spare zeme floating around somewhere that you can have.'

Kira stopped rubbing her arm and took the device, opening the side and quickly understanding how it all worked. It couldn't be simpler.

'It's not dangerous is it?'

Dylore waved her off. 'No, not at all. Like I said, it'll numb any emotions but only at the time you take it. Any emotions you feel, say an hour later, you'll need another dose for but it shouldn't be a problem.'

Kira didn't notice Skelia or the skelms when she was around the romers. Whether it be having a poole fight with Spawne and Syjet or exploring the vast hold with Dylore, she felt more comfortable and at peace…even if there was a nagging thought in her mind that it wasn't going to last forever. Therefore with this in mind she was determined to make the most of it.

When the day did finally come for them to up and leave, Kira helped them pack and then stood back and waved goodbye. There were no tears at all. The three of them had promised that they would all meet again one day and Kira knew in her heart that this was true; she had no doubt and therefore instead of being upset at their departure, she was excited at the thought of their next meeting.

Kira spent the next few seasons helping to harvest poole, playing with Forber and some of the other skelms and just fitting in, getting on with the day to day routine. In fact, it wasn't until she awoke one day to find a small cruising ship outside the cave as a gift from her parents to celebrate her fifteenth season that she realised it was time she left.

Her father slithered towards her and gave her a hug. Forber and some other skelms were standing looking at the ship.

'We know it's been hard for you growing up here when you've got so much potential inside you, so we got you this.' He waved his hand towards the ship. 'It may be old but it'll get you going, allow you to travel.'

'We got you something else too.' Her mother slithered over, trying hard not to cry as she handed over a rolled up piece of paper.

It was a brochure for The Bioricle Academy on one of Sternia's moons. The academy was a mass of giant domes covering the dull rocky surface and making it look as if the moon was infected with warts.

'You're in for six seasons, accommodation's provided. Make us proud, Kira.' Her mother hugged her so hard that she threatened to cut off her circulation.

Kira looked around. 'You make it sound as if I'm leaving right this minute?'

Her father nodded, 'why not? You have nothing holding you here, no loose ends to tie up. Your clothes and some food pills are already in the ship'

'But I'm not ready.'

Her mother smiled at her. 'Yes you are Kira...you're definitely ready.'

'And you can come back any time,' Forber called.

Kira looked around at the skelms, the caves, the marshlands and then at the battered ship and nodded in agreement. *'You're right, I am ready.'*

Having never flown a ship before it had taken a few goes to get the hang of it. The position of the seat and some of the main operating systems were adjusted as she went but the general controls were instinctive and it was only the multitude of tiny switches and lights that she would need to get accustomed to. By the time she was able to keep it steady and manoeuvre around the marshland, all the skelms were watching from the safety of their caves.

With growing ease Kira sent the ship racing across the marshlands and then began to take it upwards. She looked straight ahead and pushed the ship as hard as it would go, forcing her back into the seat. The smile on her face grew and grew until her cheeks began to ache. She was soon above the clouds and felt so free, so much older and mature. She couldn't wait to get to the Academy and find some more like her. Her heart was almost bursting with excitement at the thought.

As she slipped through the atmosphere, she held the ship steady and looked back down on Skelia in wonder, it looked so different, so insignificant. She was set now, her mind ready, and with a deep breath she turned away and flew straight on.

Domino. Protect Liberty. Protect Freedom. Protect Independence. Retrieve key.

She blinked and slowly opened her eyes. She was upright but she couldn't move. In front of her on the clear panel the same orders that had been repeating in her mind were scrolling down. Beyond that she could see torch-light and a being, not in her memory banks, looking up at her. It appeared to be only four-foot high with a scruffy piece of material around its waist. It had two arms and two legs but no head, instead the face was in the centre of the torso. The creature didn't look pleasant or welcoming. In one hand was a torch and the other held some sort of digging device. Then it attacked. The digging device hit the panel hard, cracking it and making the orders vanish. She could only close her eyes in defence as it was swung again and this time went clean through, showering her with fragments as the torch light was waved over her in examination.

Assess location.

It was clear that she was underground and the sweet but cold pungent air bought goosebumps up all over her body. She was naked.

She began to twitch and feel her muscles quickly coming to life, yet before she could start removing the sensors from her body, they were roughly yanked off by her inquisitor making her wince.

It then stepped back and turned to its right where she could see that the cave continued. It began patting the top of its torso in a fast rhythm and then called out.

'Come…here!'

She was amazed to find that she could understand what it was saying. One of her orders had been to learn local vocabulary but this was no longer necessary. The creature spoke in an earth dialect.

As she watched it was soon joined by another who looked up at her.

'Kill it…food.'

The one that had discovered her grabbed her arm and pulled her roughly out of the pod, grazing her arms on the sharp fragments and drawing blood.

Defend self. Do not die.

She landed on her feet, faced the newcomer and rammed the flat of her hand into the space between its eyes making it splutter and stagger back holding its face as the other advanced with the digging device coming down fast towards her in an arc. She slammed a fist into its wrist. Bone cracked and the device was released. She caught it and quickly assessed its weight and potential then rammed the sharp end into the centre of the creatures face causing a spray of dark green ooze. It fell back shuddering, with the weapon still embedded.

She picked up the torch and turned to the other. It was now bent over whimpering and spitting out green ooze.

50

Without a second thought she forced it upright then put the torch in its face and pushed backwards until it was pinned against the cave wall.

'Where am I?' she asked.

'No…fire…no.' It could clearly feel the fire beginning to burn through its thick skin now.

'Where?'

But it was too late. She stepped back as the fire burned through the skin and came into contact with the green ooze. The fire quickly spread through the creature. She watched for a few minutes until the creature was no more than a charred black mass and then looked around.

Find sustenance.

She picked up the other torch and waved them both around, pleased to see a reflection in one corner which meant water.

She walked over and jammed the torches in the ground before kneeling down and looking over the side at her reflection.

She was no child, yet not quite an adult. Her skin was pale and flawless, her hair long and golden. She had clear blue eyes and a slightly upturned nose. She opened her mouth to see two rows of perfect white teeth and ran her tongue along them. Satisfied with what she saw she plunged both hands into the cool water, destroying the reflection, then cupped them and bought them back to her face and took a sip of water. There were traces of potassium and calcium, but the other tastes were unknown to her. Whatever they were, however, were not toxic to her and she happily continued drinking until her thirst had been quenched.

Find clothing and transport. Continue with missions, Domino. Do NOT fail!

The auto-pilot function, although basic and only able to hold a simple course, still gave her the opportunity to flick through the welcoming brochure. It was certainly interesting, all the photos of happy, welcoming students only made her more excited and eager to get there. It was a place of infinite opportunity, a million things to discover and learn. She also had a pass-card that doubled as the key to her room and a map which at first looked impossible to decipher until she learned it was all colour-coded and according to her pass-card, she needed only stick to the green zones.

Fortunately, as she approached and saw the various entrances and exits, each with ships coming and going, the green zones made themselves clear and she easily followed the signs.

The docks were conical in shape, each with a long chimney.

Kira hovered over the top of one and then slowly let the ship fall downwards until she was inside before manoeuvring into a space, clumsily scraping the wall as she did.

She switched off the engines, gathered everything together and climbed out, looking around. There was a student heading towards the ship next to hers. She couldn't tell if it was male or female as it had no features on its pale face at all, bar two glowing eyes, but it was dressed as a young person would.

'Hi there,' she smiled and waved.

The student looked up at her, narrowed its eyes and continued walking, only slightly quicker, to its ship.

Kira shrugged and made her way to the green exit. She clearly still had a lot to learn.

Once inside she stopped and stared. She was at one end of a seemingly endless corridor that was almost as high as it was long. Lining the walls were an infinite number of multi-coloured lockers with platforms, ladders and elevators connecting them all.

There were students everywhere, so many of different sizes, shapes and colours that it was impossible to take it in. Some had long appendages meaning they could reach a high locker from the ground, while others had wings or were just able to fly without any assistance.

'Excuse me.'

Kira turned to her left to find a small booth.

Inside was an elderly woman, evident by the deep lines on her face. She wore a black tunic but her body was so thin that Kira could have easily wrapped her thumb and forefinger around one of her arms. Her head was a perfect circle with a crop of curly grey hair on top and yet when she turned to the side to check one of the screens Kira saw that her head was as flat as a disc. Her mouth was very small and pursed, a pair of spectacles sat on her minute nose.

'Can I see your pass-card please?' she asked.

'Sure,' Kira handed it to her. 'It's my first day.'

The woman ignored her and waved it over a small sensor in front of her which gave a satisfied "bleep". She looked up at Kira pursing her lips even tighter and then, not content, waved it over the sensor again only to receive the same response.

'Is anything wrong?' Kira asked.

'…No…' She passed the card back to Kira. 'It appears not…'

'Oh, great…actually I was wondering if you could-'

'Please move along.' The woman went back to the screen.

Kira did as asked, looked at the pass-card and noted her locker number, then walked along, looking up at the endless rows and columns of lockers.

Not looking where she was going, she collided with a student making him take a step forward and drop the books he was carrying.

'Koontz!'

He spun round to face her. He didn't look very happy. He was stocky and yet not much shorter than Kira but he skin was so hard and rough it looked like rock and he only had one eye in the centre of his face.

'Sorry, I wasn't looking,' Kira smiled apologetically.

He said nothing as he looked her up and down. 'You a meta?'

Kira shook her head. 'No, I'm a skelm.'

That made him grin, broadly, displaying his rough grey teeth. 'Course you are, how dumb of me.' He picked up his books and then stood to one side. 'Best be more careful in future.'

'I will, thanks.' She continued, noticing that he didn't stop watching her.

Her locker was on the second tier. She quickly made her way up the steps, still aware of the odd glance she was receiving. But then she was the new girl, so it was to be expected.

She ran her pass-card down along the slot in the front of her locker and it opened allowing her to place the bulk of her stuff inside.

She shut the locker and came face to face with herself, or so she thought. Her heart leapt. The girl standing in front of her also had dark brown skin, two hands-both with five fingers on each and black hair, tied up.

'Hi there,' the girl said.

'Hi.'

'You new?'

Kira nodded.

'Where are you from?'

'I'm from Skelia, you?'

'Earth.'

Kira looked apologetically blank. 'Don't know it.'

'You wouldn't. It's not there any more.'

Kira was now aware of more than one pair of eyes watching them. 'Not there…I don't-'

The girl began to laugh and then snapped her head back. When she bought it forwards she had changed. Her skin was now a dull orange and scaled, while her eyes were slanted and reptilian. Her short hair was shockingly pink and stylishly scruffy. She flicked out a dark green, forked tongue at Kira.

'No, it's not there any more...BOO!' She lunged at Kira.

Kira jumped and fell backwards as laughter erupted around them. She looked around, close to tears, then picked herself up and made her way back down the steps and along the corridor as everyone stood either laughing or just watching her.

When she was out of the way, she ducked into a niche and quickly gave herself a shot of zeme, then sank to the ground and let the hurt fade away.

Over the next few days it did not get any easier. That night when she returned to her ship it wouldn't start, and when she asked for help she'd had to wait three hours for someone to come and look, only to be told there was nothing they could do. She'd begged and pleaded with them and, reluctantly, as if afraid that someone might see, they'd quickly opened a side panel and fixed it before walking off in a rush.

When she got to her dorm, someone had already been there and removed all light fittings, and then someone else decided to have a loud party next door and remove any chance she had of sleeping.

In classes, she was often ignored by the teacher and found things thrown at the back of her head. A jar of poole was emptied out into her bag, spilling over her books, only for her to get the blame and be told she should take more care. By the end of the week she was becoming tired and was probably starting to overdose on zeme. The climax came during a class later that week: the lecture had become boring and she'd slipped down in her seat. As the lecturer requested that they make a note of the homework she sat up only to find that her hair was tied to the back of her chair. She cried out in pain.

The teacher stared at her and then scolded her for being disruptive.

'KOONTZ!' She screamed at the teacher as she tried to undo her hair. She had quickly learnt that this was the common swear word/curse and it had the desired effect on the teacher.

'What did you say, human?'

Human. Kira had heard someone call her that before but couldn't recall when.

'Somebody ties my hair to the chair and you have a go at me without even trying to find out who did it? That's not fair!'

'Get out of my classroom!'

The entire class was now deathly silent.

Kira undid her hair, gathered her books and got to her feet, kicking the chair back into the desk of whoever had messed with her hair. She then removed the zeme injector from her pocket in front of everyone, put it to her neck and pulled the trigger, instantly feeling her muscles begin to relax and her temper dissipate.

She put it back in her pocket and closed her eyes for a second, satisfied.

'Was that zeme?' the lecturer asked.

Kira glanced back at the lecturer as she walked towards the door. 'Yeah…'

'zeme is an illegal substance, go to the manager's office immediately.'

Kira didn't stop to close the door but she did go to the manager's office. She had some complaints of her own.

She was let straight in.

The room was a large cave. There was a window, lights overhead and even a desk and chair but the rock walls were bare and covered in slick translucent ooze.

The manager was standing running his hands through a pool of ooze that had formed in one of the crevices. He had two arms and a smart jacket on but beneath that were ten long, thin legs and a fat, grey abdomen with a crease down the centre. He also had two heads, one of which was currently asleep on his shoulder, muttering in its sleep.

He turned and crawled over to Kira before resting on his abdomen.

'Kira, isn't it? Please, take a seat.'

Kira sat down on a fancy wooden chair that looked completely out of place.

'I've been hearing a lot about you already and you've only just started.'

Kira wasn't surprised. 'As long as they told you what they've been doing to me too. It's hardly been welcoming.'

'You've also been seen taking zeme.' He frowned at her.

Kira put her hands up to protest her innocence. 'I didn't know it was illegal…it helps me, keeps me calm. There are no side-effects you know.'

'It's still illegal and as such I don't think I can let you stay here any longer.'

'What?' Kira stood up angrily. 'But I've done nothing wrong! From the first moment I walked in here, I've been picked on and yet I've never done anything to anyone.'

'I'm sorry.'

'Is it just because I'm the new girl? Because, surely that'll pass?'

The manager looked at her with pity. 'It's because you're human.'

Kira looked puzzled again. 'I keep getting called that, why? I'm a skelm.'

He spoke softly to her. *'You don't know what you are?'*

'I know I'm different to the other skelms, but-'

The manager raised a hand to silence her. 'Kira. I'm afraid there's a lot you don't know and if you stay here it's only going to get worse. Of course, all fees will be repaid in full.

Kira clenched her fists and took a step towards the door.

'Kira, before you go, I recommend you go down to the library and do some…research,' he said without looking up.

'I…'

'Go Kira…and good luck with whichever direction you choose to take.'

Kira suddenly felt dejected. She'd tried so hard, desperately hard, to fit in and be accepted. She didn't expect to suddenly become the most popular person, but to have everyone decide to dislike her just because…she was a human?

It was while walking along a corridor, narrowly avoiding a missile thrown in her direction that she'd remembered Annex calling her a human. In truth, as much as it hurt to admit it, she knew she wasn't really a skelm. Sure, there are differences in species, but only variations in shape and colour and that was usually just skin deep. She'd often hoped to discover that she was some kind of sub-species of skelm, or new evolution.

Kira made her way into the library, head down and shoulders hunched, well aware that the librarian - of the same species as the elderly lady in the entrance booth - was watching her, expecting her to try and steal or break something, finger no doubt hovering over the security button.

But Kira disappointed her and sat down peacefully at a corner booth before slipping on the headpiece and gloves and waiting for the system to adjust to her physical profile. It didn't take long. She felt the gloves begin to shrink comfortably around her hands as the headpiece adjusted itself so she could see perfectly.

As a menu came up in front of her, she raised her hands to select "History". There were millions of files, each no doubt covering many thousands of millennia in each and every galaxy or system. Not seeing what she wanted, she bought up the search menu and typed in "human".

No matches found in the Draven Galaxy.

"Expand search."

Please select Galaxy/star system.

Kira desperately tried to recall all she had ever been told. Everything anyone had ever mentioned to her that she'd ignored, convinced she was a skelm. Then she remembered something.

"Earth."

Do you mean Earth, the Milky Way?

Kira shrugged, accepted it and sat back as a short film began:

There was an image of an almighty explosion, spreading debris and matter far and wide across a vast open desert of space. The images then began to speed up and showed a single planet. It was mainly a deep blue with patches of green interspersed and Kira felt a strange longing deep within.

The video then zoomed right in to show a single creature leaping out of the water and laying on the bank, looking as if it was going to die, but then before her eyes, the creature grew legs and began walking. Then there were suddenly hundreds of them, huge terrifying reptiles roaming around and Kira was about to stop the video, thinking she had the wrong one, when a meteor hit the planet, wiping out all the reptiles and covering the world in ice. She then saw inside a cave, not unlike the ones on Skelia and saw two beings, both covered in hair and wearing the skins of animals. They looked only vaguely like her.

Then the video stopped and a voice-over began.

'These were the first humans. Innocent simple beings, content to live off the land, in harmony with their planet, their home.'

The video then began speeding up again and she saw more humans, quickly realising without a doubt that she was one. The images showed fighting, death, bloodshed and war. Strangely decorated paper rectangles were shown en masse and seemed to be very popular amongst the males as the video depicted that the more they had of this, the more they wanted.

It seemed to focus only on pale humans; the dark-skinned ones like her were usually shown behind bars or in chains. Kira found this unsettling; she didn't consider herself dangerous.

Kira found the lust for the rectangles bizarre, especially when the video then showed the planet suffering and dying, beautiful forests being cut down and animals being forced from their homes in order for the males to gain more of this paper. Soon the forests were replaced by tall buildings that scraped the sky and all filled with more males trying to gain yet more paper at the expense of everything around them.

The video then began to speak again as some males in white coats were shown celebrating something. One of them had skin the same colour as Kira's.

'Unable to cope with their overpowering emotions of lust, greed and pride, the humans tried to build their own sun. Why? It is not known.'

There was then a picture of a small blue sun in a container and more happy people. They were all cheering one man, the dark-skinned man. Next to him stood a female also dark-skinned with a hand resting on her heavily swollen stomach.

Kira paused the video and looked at the two of them. There was something so familiar in their faces.

She let the video continue. *'In the words of Timms himself, any species that destroys its very home for something it can never have is not only foolish but does not deserve to inhabit a civilised galaxy.'*

The final image was of the blue sun growing so big that it dwarfed the planet and then absorbed it.

'Humans were intelligent, there was never any question of that, but they lacked guidance and discipline. Their world was ruled by those that had too much but wanted yet more. Thus they stood no chance. The one and only thing they have contributed is The English Language. Although complicated to newcomers, it is a very clever system of letters and is now used in many galaxies.'

Kira pulled off the head set and gloves sharply. Tears poured from her eyes and she fumbled in her pocket for the zeme. It took her a few moments to insert a new cartridge and she knew she was being watched. Her face was hot now and she could feel an avalanche of emotions wanting to break free, but she couldn't handle them. She could feel how strong they were and knew she wouldn't be able to cope. Not caring who saw any more, she gave herself a shot and let go, head down between her knees waiting for the waves to subside.

She wiped her eyes and smoothed back her hair, taking deep breaths. She looked up and wasn't surprised to see the librarian with a security guard, pointing at her and talking as if she'd just attacked somebody.

Kira stuffed the zeme back in her pocket, picked up her things and headed out another door, watched constantly.

'Why didn't you tell me?'

Kira had gone straight home and now stood at the entrance to the cave barking at her mother who had come to see why she was home so soon.

'Kira?'

'Why didn't you TELL ME?' Kira thumped the cave wall, and then winced, rubbing her fist. 'Why didn't you tell me what I was? Why did you lie to me? I'm a human and everyone hates me for that. They think I'm stupid and greedy like all the rest of them.'

Her mother slithered towards her but didn't touch her. 'Kira, one day you may…become a parent…I don't know, but if you do, you'll learn how hard it is.'

'It's not difficult to tell the truth.' Kira folded her arms, she was angry and determined to win the argument.

'I've never lied to you Kira, I've always said you were different and you are.'

'Why didn't you tell me what I was?'

'It wasn't my place to. Being a parent, it's hard to stand back and let your children be exposed to the cruelty of life but it's essential for them to grow. I would have been happy to tell you but it was something you had to discover for yourself when you were old enough.'

Kira stood breathing heavily, eyes focussed on her mother, trying hard to think of a comeback. 'They were horrible to me, everyone was.'

Her mother nodded. 'I thought they would be.'

'And yet you wanted me to go?'

'Life is not always easy, Kira. By facing and overcoming these things you will become stronger.'

Now Kira bowed her head and relaxed. *'I don't want to be strong, I want to be accepted.'*

Her mother finally rested a hand on her shoulder and then bought her close to hug her. 'Kira, most species' path is already set for them. Take Forber's. He's hardly ever likely to leave Skelia and will spend most of his life farming poole before one day creating some more skelms of his own. Admittedly, he accepts that and knows no different, but your future is limitless, you're not bound by any social standings. Yes, it's going to be hard to find acceptance, but what about the romers? They accepted you and you got on fantastically with them.'

Kira nodded in agreement, head still down against her mothers chest.

Her mother whispered in her ear, *'Do you want to see your egg, Kira?'*

She looked up. 'I thought you ate them?'

'Not yours…'

Kira followed her to the back of the cave and into the labyrinth of tunnels that began there. She was glad her mother was leading as it was too easy to get lost with the only light being from the yellow fungus and the cave walls looking very similar.

Deep down in the far recesses of one cave, was an alcove.

Her mother pulled some luminous fungus from the walls and held it up so Kira could see.

The egg was nothing like skelm eggs.

Kira ran her hand over it, surprised to find it was cold and metallic. The soft cushioning inside was still intact and covered in, now dead, wires and sensors.

She then traced the wording on the side with her finger. NASA

'What's NASA?'

Her mother sighed. 'We presumed it was your name or something, we've never truly known.

Kira turned it round to look at the end. 'It's a ship of some sort; it must have come from Earth.' She span around in excitement. 'If I escaped, maybe others did too? There might be a new planet somewhere!'

Her mother once again rested a hand on her shoulder. 'Kira, we've never heard of any other humans surviving and in truth, humans when together in large numbers are not the best influence on each other.'

'What do you mean?'

'In all honesty, I hope no other humans did survive, for your sake. Humans made a lot of mistakes and without their influence; you can avoid making the same.'

'I...' Kira knew she was right but still had trouble accepting it.

'I know it's hard, but we believe you were sent into the galaxy for a reason. Perhaps it's your job to give humans a better reputation. You alone could change others opinions and redeem your race.'

Kira smiled with pride. 'That's a lot to ask of someone.'

Her mother reached down and fingered the key around her neck. 'This could well be a clue. I think it'll show its true purpose when the time is right.'

Kira rested her head against her mother's chest. 'So what do I do now?'

Resting a comforting hand on her head, her mother replied. 'Stay here with us for now, we can teach you what we know and in time I'm sure an opportunity will present itself.'

Kira closed her eyes and hugged her tightly. 'I love you mum.'

Failure.

She'd been too late and had failed to complete her first objective. With a thick length of wire she whipped her back again, hard. As the wire lashed an earlier wound, she grimaced and fought back the tears that were now stinging her eyes.

Failure is not tolerated.

Immediately upon leaving the dense cave system, still naked and killing another three creatures on the way out, she had found out where she was. It was a Buena Crystal mine and there had been a pick-up ship docked outside. She killed the two occupants, one of whom had had a similar body to hers - except for an extra couple of arms. Regardless, she had taken the clothing: a black body-suit which was loose but warm. She'd tied her long hair back with some wiring and taken the ship. She was surprised it survived her learning to drive it, but it had and she'd set off watching the in ship navigation working adjacently with her device.

Her pod had not only contained her, there had also been a small hand-held device. The screen showed a planet with a flashing green beacon on it.

However, once on the planet, she quickly realised that the beacon was the only thing left in operation.

Nine bodies, ten pods. She quickly discovered by process of elimination who it was. It had been no accident, there had been a slaughter here, and she hadn't got there fast enough to prevent it. The hand-held device was picking up no other signals so she now she had no leads or clue as to where the others were.

She lashed herself again as hard as she could.

With books bought from pick-up drivers, Kira was educated only to quickly find how little use it was.

History was interesting in the case of some planets, but the majority of it seemed to have little use for the future.

Geography was unnecessary. Even though her ship was of a basic class it still had a decent enough knowledge of the Draven Galaxy and she wouldn't be going anywhere without it.

English she found fascinating because it was an earth language. In a galaxy that loathed her kind, they had taken passionately to an earth creation. It gave her hope.

One of the many things that had interested her was buena crystals. On their own, they were completely harmless and a core part of a ship's engine. But because of the massively destructive ion power a ton of them could produce, each and every crystal was catalogued and numbered, then separately rationed. The mines were run strictly under the watchful eye of the Contra.

The biological make-up of each species was long and tiresome but interesting. Especially when she learnt that humans are the only known species that don't lay eggs; the young grow inside the mother. Kira had laughed about that at first until she recalled the image in the library of the dark-skinned woman with the swollen stomach and quickly gave herself some zeme before any unwanted thoughts invaded her mind.

Mathematics and physics she found to be completely useless, even the primitive skelms had machines that could do calculations for them. Her mother had argued that machines could break down and go wrong, but Kira had just come to the conclusion that there were a million and one things to fill the mind with and maths was not a high priority.

The only other thing she did spend time learning was basic ship maintenance. The last thing she wanted, especially with her ship, was to break down on some remote asteroid and not be able to replace the Lemurian Generator Core. The maintenance book also taught her about ship classes: Alpha ships were small, quick and lightweight - much like her own, Beta ships were akin to The Genesis only not usually with so many armaments, or a bastard crew of pirates. The Gamma class spoke for itself.

Seasons once again passed by. The harvest came, followed by the storms and then during the following harvest in Kira's seventeenth season, her father had an idea.

'You should join The Contra.'

The Contra was the policing force in the Draven Galaxy. Her father explained that the Contra were always looking for new members and, unlike The Academies, saw everyone as equal, even humans...or so her father had heard.

Kira took him up on his offer, packed her things and headed for the Dali Moon, where the recruiting base and training centres were based.

Circling the Dali Moon was an imposing armada of Beta class crafts. The moon itself was a mass of dense golden forest amid purple and red rock mountains.

The Contra HQ was located in an enormous clearing at the base of a red mountain fringed by forest.

As Kira flew overhead, following the signs for new recruits, the area surrounding the buildings looked like a giant playground with all sorts of training apparatus, and all currently occupied by a variety of species.

She parked her ship with the other new recruits and joined the crowd.

There were no introductions, no forms to be filled out and no friendly smiling faces either. Instead, she was merely lead along a slim corridor, passing sensors which changed from red to green as each person passed by. The corridor was slim enough to ensure that no one could walk by the side of anyone else. At the end, they were all given a small bundle of clothes - depending on the species, and a weapon. The recruits were then taken to changing rooms already occupied by a multitude of species either in the process of changing or already leaving for the training areas.

The loose-fitting bodysuit was purple and red camouflage, clearly designed to blend into the surrounding mountains. The boots were plain black and the weapon was a basic blaster, nothing special - even Forber had one.

Pretty soon, Kira was standing in the second line of three rows of ten as their instructor paced up and down looking at them. He wasn't particularly tall. He was slim and his entire body looked as if it had been stretched, even his head was long and ended in a flat bald top. But his eye was sharper than the two long claws that protruded from each of his forearms.

'So let me guess...' He began to speak as if talking to himself, but loud enough for them to hear. 'You want the easy way? I wonder how many of you were having too much fun while at the Academy only to forget to study, and now you're stuck. Can't get a job? Parents don't want you around any more? Or maybe you passed through the Academy with excellence, had a great job, but got bored. Either way you've ended up here and now you want to join The Contra.' He put his hands behind his back and strolled along the rows, staring straight upwards. 'Well I can tell you now that The Contra doesn't want you. In fact I'm willing to bet that out of these three rows; only one at the most, will get to wear the uniform and help police Draven Galaxy.' He stopped and stared at them all. 'You are not holiday. You will be pushed to the limit and within the first few days we will see blood, sweat and tears from you. If any of you are actually serious about joining, you'll fight through it. A lot of species don't want to be arrested or caught and will not go easily, so believe me when I say that this is nothing to what you will face *if* successful.' He relaxed his shoulders and took a deep breath. 'Of course, no official paperwork's been signed so you're under no obligation to stay. Any time you feel you can't take it any more, leave. Your ship will be right where you left it and you can even keep the bodysuit so long as you don't come back.' He stood watching in perfect silence, clearly used to at least one person dropping out early, but nobody did. Half surprised, he snapped his claws open and shut before continuing. 'My name is Instructor Dalle and any abbreviators will be punished.'

They followed him as he gave them a guided tour of the facility. The expansive training grounds where actual dangerous prisoners were used, shooting ranges, and the barracks that each held ten bunk-beds.

This is where Instructor Dalle left them. 'You don't have to go to sleep but I recommend it. You're not allowed out of the barracks until you're collected in the morning at first light. Sleep well.' And with that he left.

Kira lay on her bunk and looked around to see that a few recruits stayed awake chatting and getting to know the new faces, or played an odd game with tiny clouds in the palms of their hands that emitted thunder strikes to the loser, but the rest got into bed and slept.

Kira wasn't tired, had no idea how to play the thunder-game, and was of no interest to anyone so she stared at the metal rungs of the bunk above her with her hands behind her head and let her mind wander…

'Hey!'

Kira opened her eyes to see one of the other recruits prodding her. She knew by the large shell on his back and the beak that he was a tortle.

'What?'

He pressed his pincers to her lips as he looked around. *'Ssssh! It's night time now.'*

Kira pushed the pincer away then sat up and looked around. It was silent both inside the bunker and outside. She must have dozed off.

'What do you want?' she asked.

'You want to come and look around outside?'

'We're not supposed-'

He waved her off. *'Oh please, you're not allowed to do a lot of things in life, but that doesn't stop you doing them, does it?'*

Kira smiled. *'We're here to join a policing force you know.'*

'Yes, and zeme is highly illegal here...hypocrite.'

Kira quickly put a hand to the pocket on her thigh.

'Relax, I wouldn't take it. So, you coming or what?'

'Yeah, might as well.'

He lead the way and she followed. Noticing he had his blaster, she grabbed hers too.

There were a few guards wandering around, but they were watching the skies and the mountains, clearly more worried about an attack than two new recruits sneaking out.

They edged past the barracks, slipped beneath a guard-tower while the searchlight was in the mountains, and then vaulted a fence and found themselves in the forest.

'So what's your name?' he asked her, wandering along in front of her taking swipes at the foliage with his pincers.

'Kira.'

'Mine's Angelo. Why'd you join up?'

Kira shrugged. 'It was my dad's idea.'

'Your adoptive dad, you mean...yeah?'

Kira turned to look at a plant creeping stealthily up a tree as he spoke. 'Something like that.'

'Ah relax,' he waved a pincer in the air nonchalantly. 'It's nothing to be ashamed of. You know, humans were pretty smart, they invented nano-technology, or at least the original concept.'

'Well, they're dead now; I try not to think about them.'

Angelo held up his pincers in understanding. 'Hey, no problem...' He rammed a pincer into a nearby tree and gouged a chunk out. 'My dad made me come here too, thinks it'll be good for character building. You see, I was like a teacher at my Academy. Not officially or anything, but I took it upon myself to help the shy and insecure kids to adjust to the world.'

'That was good of you.'

'Exactly! But no one else saw it that way, they called me a thug. The galaxy's a pretty rough place and these shy kids are going to get hit sooner or later, so I figured that by being rough on them, stealing credits, disabling their ships, they'd be able to adjust easier. Course, did anyone see it that way? No. I never beat anyone up too badly, just the odd few punches here and there...'

Kira listened as he spoke, but she was starting to wish she'd stayed in bed. He was clearly deluded.

'...So, everyone got mad, told my parents I was abusing younger kids and dad packs me off to this place. Thanks Dad.'

'Maybe the kids didn't want to adjust,' Kira said. 'Maybe they weren't ready to be introduced to the rigours of life just yet. After all, everyone's different.'

He scoffed at her. 'Sheesh, who died and made you Timm?'

'Timm?' Kira had heard that name mentioned before, but couldn't place it.

'Yeah Timm, you know? All seeing powerful force that watches over the Draven Galaxy. Timm the Almighty, Timm the Supreme?'

'Never heard of him.'

'Ah, you humans probably had something different.'

Kira was about to turn and head back, when Angelo froze and put a pincer to his beak indicating for her to be silent.

He looked at the bushes to his left and then began to duck down. Suddenly he dove into the bush.

There was a series of high-pitched squeaks as he struggled with something that clearly didn't want to be struggled with, before standing back up triumphantly, holding a small, thin reptile tightly in his pincers. The creature was no longer than a foot and was a sandy-yellow colour with brown spikes down its back. But the strangest thing about it was a thick metal collar around its neck which looked very cumbersome on the frail creature.

'It's a pavouk,' Angelo said, holding it up to show her.

'Very nice,' Kira said with a sigh.

'What's this?' Angelo noticed the collar and ran his pincer over it, only for the creature to begin panicking and struggling to get free.

'I'm tired, let's head back.' Kira yawned and stretched. 'Dalle did say we had to be up at first light.'

'I just want to see what this collar does.'

The pavouk was now going crazy, clearly not keen on anyone touching the collar. Consequently Angelo was having a hard time holding onto it.

'Keep still you little-'

'I don't think it wants you to do that.' Kira said, taking a couple of steps towards him. 'Best let it go.'

'In a minute.'

Kira could see the creature wasn't just panicking, it was terrified. She grabbed Angelo's wrist and held him back. 'Leave it alone!'

He turned his attention to Kira, snatched his pincer from her and then rammed it in her stomach, winding her and knocking her to her knees where she fought for breath.

'It's just a pavouk, you know? They don't have parents or families, no one'll miss it. What's the big deal?'

Without thinking, Kira grabbed her blaster and, with one hand still on her stomach, pointed it at him. 'Let it go!'

'You're nuts.' Then he smiled. 'You won't shoot me, you're a human. I know for a fact that humans only kill other humans, and then only for credits.'

He began to laugh and Kira placed her finger on the trigger

He ignored her and went back to fiddling with the pavouk's collar as it stopped struggling and started squeaking pitifully.

'Humans…soft on the outside, softer on the inside.'

Kira was about to say something when there was a blast of hot plasma. Angelo released the pavouk and fell backwards onto his shell where he rocked for a few moments.

Kira dropped the gun in horror and froze as the pavouk stood on its hind legs watching her.

'It was sensitive! The trigger was more sensitive than I thought it would be.' She spoke to the reptile, unaware of whether or not it understood.

'It came from over here!'

Kira's breath caught in her throat as she heard guards coming their way. She quickly crawled over to Angelo to see how badly wounded he was.

She turned away, feeling ill. It had been a direct head-shot. He wasn't going to pull through.

As the bushes near them began to rustle, the pavouk quickly ran towards her. Before she could stop it, it crawled inside her bodysuit and lay flat against her stomach.

She was just about to protest and fetch it back out when two guards burst through the bushes. Silence reigned for a few moments as they assessed the scene before them.

They turned to Kira. 'On your feet!' the shorter one ordered her.

They both held much larger blasters than Kira's so she didn't argue.

'It was an accident.'

'Kick the blaster towards us.'

Kira did as she was told. They checked it, and then looked at Angelo. 'Doesn't look like an accident, that's some precise shooting.'

'He was upsetting a pavouk.'

One guard smiled, the other did not. 'You shot him for upsetting a pavouk?' He snarled with distaste at her. 'Where I come from, pavouks are a delicacy. I've eaten loads. You gonna kill me too?'

'No, of course not, look-'

'Turn around and put your hands behind your back.'

'Listen, I was-'

'NOW!'

Kira did as instructed and then one guard kept his blaster on her while the other came over, grabbed her wrists and cuffed them together.

'Always knew you humans were bloodthirsty,' he whispered to her. *'You should have died with the rest of them.'*

Kira said nothing.

Four walls, one tiny window, and a ledge with a couple of tatty blankets tossed on it. Kira was unceremoniously pushed into her new home and then left alone as the heavy door slammed shut behind her.

The first thing Kira did was check there were no cameras visible. She then grabbed the zeme from her pocket and take a shot, instantly quelling the emotions of frustration and rage that had been building up.

She felt something move inside her body suit and panicked before remembering the pavouk.

It undid a couple of the buttons and peered out, before crawling down her leg and jumping up onto the ledge. It watched at her as she sat down on the floor, back against the wall.

'You best run. You heard him; he eats the likes of you.'

The pavouk continued watching her for a moment before speaking. 'Thank you.'

Kira looked up in shock, wondering where the voice had come from, before realising and shifting her attention to the creature.

'You can talk?'

It nodded.

'Well, that's great, you can tell them it was an accident.'

It shook its head. 'pavouk's can't talk; I'm not like the others. If they hear me speak…they'll start asking questions.' It touched the collar as it spoke, as though needing reassurance that it was still there.

'Great. Looks like we're stuck here then.' Kira sighed and rested her head back against the wall.

'No, they'll let us out tomorrow when they put you to death.'

Kira snapped her head forward. 'What?'

'You murdered a recruit for The Contra on Contra ground; they're hardly likely to let you go with a caution.'

'But I didn't murder him…not exactly!'

'They won't see it any other way.'

Kira put her head in her hands and closed her eyes.

'My name's Cesar.'

Kira said nothing.

'What's your name?'

'Is there really any point to this line of chatter? We're both going to be dead in the morning.'

Cesar lay down on the blanket still watching her. 'Technically *I'm* not charged with murder.'

Kira looked up. 'True, but you are a delicacy.'

'Oh…yes.'

'My name's Kira, if you must know. The last human and therefore disliked wherever I go just because of what "my kind" did.'

'I don't dislike you.'

Kira gave him a half-smile. 'You don't know me.'

'You saved my life, didn't you?'

Kira gave another half-smile as she looked around the cell. 'Only temporarily.'

'We're innocent, Timm will help us out.'

'Yeah?' Kira pulled herself to her feet and headed for the ledge. 'I keep hearing that name, but I've yet to see any evidence of him.' She sat down next to the pavouk and took one of the blankets.

He moved over to let her lie down and then sat on her chest. 'Let's make a deal: if we get out of this alive, you have to believe in and have faith in Timm.'

Kira laughed softly. 'Deal.' She made herself comfortable before motioning to his collar. 'What is that? Looks pretty unwieldy.'

Cesar looked somewhat embarrassed at the mention of it. 'You ever heard of Annex?'

Kira nodded slowly, visibly swallowing as she did.

'Well he likes to experiment…and there you go.'

'So what does it do?'

'It's not something I like to discuss.' He changed the subject. 'What's that around *your* neck?'

Kira fingered the key. 'I don't know. I presume it's the key to *something*. I've had it all my life.'

'You were bought up on Skelia, right?'

Kira nodded. 'How'd you know?'

'I have a highly developed sense of smell…you smell of poole.'

Kira bought her armpit up to her face and sniffed. 'I do?'

Cesar smiled. 'Only to creatures with a highly developed sense of smell.'

Kira took a deep breath and yawned. 'Well, Cesar, I'm tired so I'm going to try and get some sleep…tomorrow should be interesting.'

'Have faith Kira.'

But she was already asleep.

The Contra were certainly punctual.

Kira was rudely awakened long before her body was ready and had to be dragged out of the cell. She could feel Cesar once again inside her suit, resting against her stomach.

She was taken out into a clearing where over half the recruits stood watching. There was a metal pole sticking up out of the ground in the centre, about two feet taller than her. No fancy mechanisms were necessary, just a simple pair of handcuffs that bound her wrists behind the pole as she stood facing Instructor Dalle.

'Kira. You are charged with the brutal and lethal killing of a fellow recruit. How do you plead?'

'It was an accident.'

'Evidence shows otherwise. The blaster used one round and it was a perfect head-shot. Too perfect for an accident.'

Kira said nothing; she just silently gazed along the lines of recruits, most looking at her as if death was the best thing for her. No one seemed to be inclined to defend her.

'Nothing to say in your defence?' Dalle asked.

'I was there, you weren't,' Kira spoke, not just to Dalle but to everyone. 'I know I'm innocent and was acting out of consideration for a weaker creature so my conscience is clear.'

Dalle nodded, trying to understand. 'Yes, the pavouk. However, no pavouk was found in the forest.'

Kira was about to encourage Cesar to show his face when she remembered what he had said about "public appearances". She had little choice now but to trust in Timm. *'I'm innocent,'* she said and hung her head with a sigh, waiting.

'Kira, with no evidence to back up your story and the violent history of your race, I have no choice but to charge you with murder and sentence you to immediate execution.'

A solitary tear ran down Kira's cheek and dropped to the dusty ground below as she heard blasters being loaded and silence hung in the air.

Suddenly, the silence was shattered by the engine of a ship that hovered overhead and began to descend as recruits moved out of the way and covered their faces from the billowing dust.

Kira looked up to see a brand new, black and silver Alpha class come to a rest behind the firing squad who had turned their attention from her to the newcomer.

Dalle looked from her to the ship and then back again, clearly still wanting to get on with the execution, but as the ship opened his attention was stolen for good by the visitor.

With the dust still in the air, Kira couldn't see what was going on and had to keep blinking to keep her eyes clear. She also felt Cesar take a quick look out of her bodysuit, obviously wondering why they were still both alive.

The next thing she saw was Instructor Dalle walking towards her with a look of hatred on his face. He went behind her and set her free.

'You have friends in high places…human.'

She ignored him as someone else walked through the settling dust towards her.

'Spawne?'

He looked completely different to when she had last seen him. He hadn't aged much but his black hair was now specked with white and he wore a stunningly smart white and silver suit.

'Look at you, Kira. You're all grown up.'

Kira could only smile as a mixture of relief and an all new spark of faith erupted deep inside her.

'Your timing's good.'

'Let's get out of here.' He took her hand and led her away from the post, past the firing squad and into his ship as the recruits watched, many with open mouths.

As the ship lifted off, Kira sat down in the co-pilots seat next to Spawne and took a deep breath, then gave herself a shot of zeme and relaxed. 'What about my ship?' she asked.

'Forget it.'

Cesar let himself out of her bodysuit and perched on her lap.

'You've got a pet?' Spawne asked, noticing Cesar.

'I'm no pet, I'm her friend,' Cesar replied. 'And thanks to you she now believes in Timm.'

Spawne looked impressed. 'She does?'

Kira had her eyes closed but nodded. 'Yeah…she does.'

Spawne turned his attention forward as they left the atmosphere. 'She doesn't know the half of it…'

They travelled to a far corner of the galaxy that, like much of Draven, was still unbeknownst to Kira. When Spawne began to slow the ship, Kira sat forward and looked out of the front window, mouth agape.

'*Wow*…'

Spawne smiled,. 'Yeah, things have changed.'

Ahead lay a colossal white Gamma class, with a similar one still under construction alongside. Kira had seen many ships but was finding it hard to fathom the existence of one so immense. The two ships were surrounded by a legion of Beta's and Alpha's. All were brand new and each was white, grey or silver.

'That's the *Sagittarius*,' Spawne pointed to the main ship. 'And that one, when finished, will be the *Leo*.'

'So, was all that junk in the back of your old ship valuable or something?' Kira asked, still taking in the sight of the fleet.

Spawne just smiled as he headed for a docking bay in the Sagittarius.

The interior was as pristine as the hull and immediately upon arrival, two beings, also dressed in white and silver, albeit not as lavishly as Spawne, came up to their ship and began checking it over and helping the three of them disembark.

As they walked along a corridor, Kira elbowed Spawne, 'when are you going to let on? The suspense is getting to me now.'

'Very well.' Spawne slowed to a stroll, gave a brief hand-signal to a creature they passed and took a deep breath. 'About four seasons ago, Dad was visited by Timm in his sleep. He told him that a black hole had appeared on the edge of the galaxy and it was growing. According to Timm, there is an evil inside, older than any galaxy, called Hanaan. Hanaan is feeding on all the discourse in the galaxy, the bad feelings and negativity. When satisfied, he will destroy the Draven Galaxy and all in it and not even Timm will be able to stop him. Thus why Timm encouraged my father to start what you see before you: the Centuria.'

'So you're building an army?' Cesar asked, now perched on Kira's shoulder.

Spawne shook his head. 'Not at all, an army creates death and destruction which would only feed Hanaan and make him stronger. The Centuria are committed to peace between all races and species. At first, Dad started preaching and offering help as he travelled. The first cases were so successful that many are still here today and word spread around the galaxy unbelievably fast...its growing bigger than my father ever imagined.'

They passed a room with a glass wall. Inside were a variety of beings, all dressed in simple grey robes. They

87

were lying on metallic tables, each with a red wire and a blue wire going into their heads. Every so often one of them would either grimace or smile contentedly.

'This is the preliminary purging system - note the simple grey robes,' Spawne said. 'Each time they think a negative thought, the red wire gives them a shock. Whereas if they think of a positive, pleasant thought, the blue wire will give them a rush of endorphins. Over time, they will be cured of all negativity. They will then be given silver robes and spend ten seasons in quiet prayer and reflection. Finally, they will become a white preacher and help the newcomers.'

Kira nodded in agreement, understanding, but not wishing to take part. 'Have you done that?'

Spawne shook his head. 'No, there's no need. Dad, Syjet and I have no negativity in us. All the beings you see here have come of their own free will. But it's not free. By joining the Centuria, you give up everything you own.'

'They're paying for that?' she asked.

'It's not like that. Once here, you stay for life, learning, finding inner-peace and never want for anything. Once the Leo is complete, the power and reach the Centuria will have…will…well; Dad will be numero-uno in the galaxy.'

'And that will be a good thing, right?' Kira looked at the beings on the tables again.

'Of course. No more wars or fighting, no disharmony, everyone accepting and tolerating everyone else…even humans.'

That got Kira's attention.

Spawne smiled. 'Dads kept an eye on you. In time you'll be able to go anywhere and just be accepted, no one will treat you any differently. How's that sound?'

Kira nodded. 'Yeah…it sounds good.' She couldn't help but smile.

'How did you persuade The Contra to let Kira go?' Cesar asked.

'The leaders of the Contra are members. Many have seen so much fighting and anger in their lives that they can no longer bottle it up. We're helping them to release it slowly and cleanse themselves deep within. In return, if Dad needs a favour or protection, he only has to ask. Most of the Alpha and Beta ships you saw outside are owned by the Contra…but in time, the Contra will become obsolete. The latest figures indicate that the Centuria is fast gaining more power and respect than the Contra, so much so that forty-five percent of beings now come to us when they're in trouble or need help. We're a dazzling light in the cold galaxy.'

'And what happens to the criminals?' Cesar asked, now just as interested as Kira.

'It depends. If a criminal shows a want for redemption, they can join us. If however, they show no interest in reform or rehabilitation, they will be cast into the black hole with Hanaan which may sound foolish but it stops any more negativity leaking from or being produced by that being.'

Kira thought for a moment as they passed a gigantic indoor tropical forest. Various beings in grey robes strolled around inside. 'Is there a way of showing allegiance, without having wires stuck in your head?'

'I had a feeling you were going to ask that and the answer's yes. All you need do is dye a strip of your hair white,' he turned to her and gently pulled away half her fringe. 'Just this bit would do, and then wherever you go, you'll be recognised as a member of the Centuria.' He released her hair. 'Any further questions?'

Kira nodded. 'Do you have a spare bed? I'm beat!'

Whether it was a combination of the peaceful serenity of the ship and the comfortable bed or the fact that she'd had such a tiring day, Kira slept like the dead. Completely lost to time and existence. Far away from them all.

During the sleep she awoke but only somewhat. Her body was still comatose, but her mind became aware and she could sense that she wasn't alone. There was someone sitting on the bed next to her, stroking her hair affectionately and speaking very softly to her. The visitor's voice was so quiet that she couldn't make out any words but she found it soothing and quickly slipped back into the endless void of sleep.

When she finally awoke, she still wasn't alone.

Syjet was standing by one of the windows looking out as Cesar perched on the end of the bed watching Kira sleep.

Syjet was wearing a similar style of clothing to her brother's, albeit, more feminine and flowing. Her orange hair was also much longer and now had streaks of white in it too.

'Welcome back Kira,' Cesar said. 'You've been asleep for days.'

'I have?' Kira put a hand to her forehead and then pushed her hair from her face.

'Ignore him Kira,' Syjet said, turning from the window. 'He's winding you up.'

Kira did as recommended and gave her a smile. 'Syjet, how are things?'

She turned back to the window. 'Oh you know, as exciting as being stuck in one place can be.'

Kira sat up. 'Sounds to me like you're doing a great thing here.'

'I know, I know,' Syjet nodded, not wanting to sound unappreciative. 'But I miss the roaming, the different planets, and the variety of species. Each day was completely different and there was a new challenge or adventure every time we docked. Mum wouldn't have liked this. Of course she would have been pleased with what Dad's doing, but she'd have got bored quickly and either insists he gives it up or she'd go off on her own. She was like that, as much as she loved the three of us, she was strong enough to go off on her own at any time. I wish I could go and carry on exploring the galaxy instead of spending all my time here preaching and helping people.'

'Helping people is a "good" thing, Syjet,' Cesar said with a hint of sarcasm.

'What's perked you up?' Kira asked Cesar. 'Yesterday you were scared of your own shadow. Today you're experimenting with wit?'

'Yesterday I was going to be eaten...'

'It can still be arranged, we serve a variety of species here,' Syjet warned him, with a faint smile. 'As for you Kira, you'd better get ready.'

'Why?'

'You're going hunting with Spawne.'

Two Centurian employees led Kira to the docking bay. She had borrowed some boots, comfortable black trousers and a grey top and jacket from Syjet. Her hair was tied back and Cesar was perched on her shoulder.

Once there she saw that Spawne had changed out of his regal suit and was also dressed in dark clothing.

Once inside his ship, seated and ready for take-off, Cesar left them to have a look around as Kira took the co-pilots seat.

'Syjet says we're going hunting?' she asked.

Spawne nodded. 'Yep, bounty hunting.'

On the way, Spawne explained that his father had recommended this. Groups like the Contra and private companies across the galaxy paid good money for the live capture of criminals. Spawne had been on a couple previously and developed a taste for it.

Today's target was a high profile serial killer called Hanbel: wanted by at least ten civilised planets and last seen hiding on a planet now known as Toxica 7. This had once been a buena crystal mining planet, until the diggers had gone too deep and released poisonous chemicals into the atmosphere, killing all the inhabitants. The chemicals had eventually diffused in the ozone and Toxica 7 was considered safe but the tourist industry had no interest in a planet devoid of life. It was a ghost planet.

'I'm afraid you won't get to see any action today, Kira. I need you to stay in the ship and watch my back. Hanbel's part robot and part grievian - a bad combination.'

Kira had researched grievians. They were very agile and had two legs and four arms, or two arms and four legs depending on the situation. Their genetic make-up made them easily adaptable. As with most races they were harmless and content to stay within the boundaries of the law, well, most of them were, but there's a black schneep in every family.

'Hanbel's been incarcerated twice now,' Spawne said. 'The first time he escaped easily, the second time, he got out and took plenty with him. He had a gang for a while, but once you've had a taste for blood…he was soon alone again and would just roam indiscriminately, killing when and who he pleased. We know nothing of his background but it's unlikely he'll be interested in rehab.'

'Why not just kill him?' Kira asked.

Spawne almost choked. 'Kill him? I've got no right to take another's life…' He gave her a concerned look. 'I'd heard about the human blood lust but, considering your upbringing, didn't think you'd exhibit it.'

Kira sighed. 'I didn't mean it like that. I meant, why capture him only to give him to Hanaan when it would just be quicker and easier to "take him out" now.'

'Again, because I can't do that. Criminals fear Hanaan and with good reason: they know he's going to make them suffer worse than we or the Contra will. At least that's how dad explained it to me.'

'Toxica 7, dead ahead.' Cesar said as he appeared in a duct above their heads.

Kira felt pity for the planet already. Dark, moody clouds roamed the sky like an unwelcome gang looking for trouble. To Kira the planet was much like a creature that had been beaten and kicked so many times it had given up. Dotted heavily around the rocky landscape were caves from which ran tracks, many rusting and eroded. Digging equipment, run-down housing and even the odd skeleton completed the scenery.

Spawne slowly hovered over the landscape, watching a screen in front of him as he did. Patience wasn't necessary. A "blip" soon appeared accompanied by a heat signature. He checked the readings and smiled. 'Gotcha.'

Carefully, he bought the ship down on a large plateau next to a cave entrance and then left his seat and went into the rear, returning with what looked like a gun.

He saw Kira's look and shook his head. 'It's a net-gun. Fires an unbreakable net that administers tranquillisers on impact.' He pointed to the controls in front of her. 'Keep an eye on the screen. My dot will be blue. If anything happens, leave immediately and don't look back…but I wouldn't worry.' He gave her a confident smile then left.

Kira watched through the front wind shield as he jogged over to the cave entrance ignoring the battering wind, gun slung over his shoulder, and then vanished inside. She turned her attention to the screen and watched the blue dot moving slowly around in the emptiness.

'Nice place…reminds me of home,' Cesar said, now perched on the control panel looking out.

'Really?' Kira asked.

'No, not really, pavouks don't have a home planet. Eggs are laid on the outside of ships and then subsequently get spread around. We're not exactly popular.'

'I take it yours was laid on The Genesis?' Kira enquired, now looking outside with him.

Cesar nodded. 'It was…' He fingered the collar again in contemplation.

Kira was tempted to probe further, but let it be. Instead she found herself looking outside, imagining what Earth had been like. The pictures she had seen in the library gave her a clue but it had been confusing. Planets and moons in the Draven Galaxy normally consisted of just one type of terrain. But Earth seemed to have vast cities, mountains, jungles and oceans. All sorts of planets mixed into one. It sounded fascinating. No matter what you felt like doing, the terrain was there for you.

'Kira!'

'Huh?'

Wake up, the blue dot's gone!' Cesar was pointing anxiously at the screen.

Kira looked at it, and then scanned further. Nothing. She felt her stomach knot and tighten as her heart began to beat faster.

'We have to get out of here,' Cesar said.

'We can't just leave him, Cesar.'

'Well you can't go in there after him.'

Instinctively, Kira took a quick shot of zeme and then left the cockpit and headed towards the rear.

'This is a bad idea!' Cesar called after her.

She didn't reply.

Cesar jumped down onto the pilot's chair, then to the floor and ran out to the rear to find her. She was now trying to work out how the net-gun operated, clearly getting more and more frustrated.

'Oh Koontz, I'll figure it out as I go...' Kira let the gun hang at her side and opened the rear cargo door.

'*Koontz!*' Cesar sighed before quickly scampering up her back and onto her shoulder.

'Where are you going?' she asked, pausing by the door.

'With you. I can't fly this thing, so I might as well go down in flames.'

Kira smiled then made her way down the ramp and outside. With the gun in front of her, she jogged towards the cave entrance. The wind turned her tied-back hair into a whip that began to assault Cesar until he grabbed it and held it in place. Once inside, she stopped and crouched down then looked around. The only light came from the cave entrance and all it revealed was a vast network of girders, pulleys and platforms stretching both far ahead and above her, but now redundant.

'I hope you have a plan,' Cesar whispered to her.

'I do.' She slowly walked forward, scrutinising all about for movement, and wishing she'd bought a torch.

Suddenly, there was a loud crash to her right accompanied by some strange laughter that sounded both mechanical and delirious.

The laughter didn't stop, but it was coming from high up.

Kira went to see what had caused the crash, hoping it wouldn't be what she feared.

Her fears were justified.

'Spawne…'

Spawne was a mass of deep cuts and slices, his eyes closed. There were no signs of life.

The hideous laughter now grew even more intense and began to move rapidly across one of the many platforms above her.

Kira temporarily swallowed her emotions back down and aimed the gun above her but it was pointless, she couldn't see a thing.

'A human?' The mechanical voice came from her far left now and she span round to be faced with more darkness.

'A *human…!'*

Kira aimed the gun at where she presumed the voice was coming from and watched intently.

'Not a very smart human though…'

Kira was about to reply when there was a flash of light and something green flew towards her. Before she could dive out of the way, the netting wrapped itself tightly around her and she felt a dozen pinpricks, quickly sending her to the ground and to sleep.

Cesar had leapt down from her shoulder just in time and stood behind her watching. If Hanbel attacked her, he would have just one option and the thought of it sent shivers right through him.

But Hanbel seemed to have had his fill of murder for now and suddenly dashed towards the entrance.

Cesar immediately saw his plan and ran after him.

As predicted, the killer dashed nimbly on his six legs over to the ship and scampered up into the rear.

Cesar wasn't as fast but, sure that he wasn't being followed, Hanbel was in no rush to leave and so Cesar had plenty of time to make it up the ramp and into the ship. He made his way to the cockpit to see Hanbel already initiating the engines. Cesar took a deep breath and stood back against the wall. There was only one option now. With trembling hands he reached around to the back of the collar and released it.

Kira's head was thumping as reality resurfaced around her. It was as if she'd been mentally dropped in poole and was now trying to wipe it away and recall what had happened. Fortunately, it didn't take long and she realised she was still in the net, tightly bound and unable to move.

'I'm sorry, I'm so sorry...'

'Cesar?' She tried to move her head to see where his voice was coming from.

'I'm sorry Kira, I had no choice...'

She couldn't see him but he sounded distraught and terrified.

'Where's Hanbel?'

'I didn't want to. You have to believe me.'

'Can you get me out?' Kira realised there was little point in whispering.

He didn't answer but she felt him crawl up her leg and search for the release mechanism. He found it and the net went slack.

Kira wriggled free of the netting then knelt up. Cesar was huddled up in a ball, shivering.

'What's wrong?'

Cesar didn't respond.

Kira gently touched one of his ear. It startled him and he bared his teeth at her.

'Hey!' Then she realised what it was. 'Where's your collar?'

No answer, he only wrapped himself up into a tighter ball.

'Alright, wait here.' She stood up and gazed around but the darkness swallowed everything. Finally, switching on her common sense, she left the cave and ran back towards the ship to find a torch - something she should have done initially. Then she saw something by the rear ramp and headed over, hoping it was the collar. It wasn't.

'No way…'

It was a robotic arm, still occasionally twitching. The shoulder was an ugly mess of tissue and blood, as though the arm had been ripped away.

She ran up the ramp and stopped dead, mouth agape. Hanbel was dead.

In a way, it was kind of ironic that a lethal, sadistic serial killer had met his demise in this way and she was glad he had been half robot. Robotic remains she could handle. She took a deep breath and stepped over a brown, fleshy lump. The floor was slick with some kind of ooze and she tried to keep her feet. Kira found the collar, coated in gunk and gingerly picked it up. She didn't understand what had happened here, nor was she sure she wanted to, but she figured Cesar might at least come back to his old self if he had the collar.

Back in the cave, Cesar hadn't moved an inch; he was still curled up in a tight ball. Very carefully, Kira eased the collar around his neck and then quickly snapped it shut before he could protest.

He panicked for a second and jumped up, teeth and claws bared. Then the weight of the collar jostling around as he jumped instantly calmed him and he stroked the collar affectionately.

The next thing Kira knew, he had crawled up her body and now lay curled against the back of her neck.

She decided to let him be and took a much-needed shot of zeme as she made her way over to Spawne.

She hated lying to Dylore, especially when he was down on his knees cradling what remained of his son in his arms. Syjet knelt next to him, sobbing her eyes out. But Kira had little choice.

'Hanbel just…combusted. He was boasting about not being taken alive, or something. Spawne bought him on board and…'

Dylore nodded, he clearly wasn't really listening and Kira couldn't blame him, plus there was plenty of evidence still on board to back up what she was saying. Kira left them alone.

Spawne's remains were cremated and then scattered out into the galaxy so he could continue to roam as they once had.

The funeral was attended only by Syjet, Dylore and Kira; even Cesar had been told to stay behind.

'Goodbye Son,' Dylore said as he watched the ashes flutter out into space. 'May Timm always guide you on your travels.'

'Bye Spawne, say hello to Mum for me.' Syjet sniffed back some more tears as her father held her close.

Kira had already had one shot of zeme as the ashes had been released but she could feel another surge of emotions on the way.

When they were unable to see the ashes any more and had each said their own individual farewells, they returned to their quarters.

As their rooms were in the same sector, Dylore and Kira walked along in silence, both contemplating.

'Kira?' Dylore broke the silence. 'Can I ask a favour of you?'

Kira nodded, 'sure.'

Dylore laid a hand on her shoulder. 'Thank you. Please, follow me.' He lead her back to his room which, for the owner of two expansive Gamma ships, was identical to everyone else's, and very understated. The only personal possession was a photo of the four of them next to his bed. A happy family.

'Take a seat.' He pointed to the bed as he walked over to a cupboard and began rummaging.

Kira sat down as he found what he was looking for and brought over a syringe with what looked like poole inside. H rested it next to the photo.

'How would you like to work for me, full time?' he asked her.

Kira sighed. 'I appreciate the offer, but all this purging and the white robes, well, it isn't me, sorry.'

Dylore shook his head. 'No, I need a Bounty Hunter.'

'Well....'

'I know there are a lot of Bounty Hunters out there, but you'll be employed exclusively by me. You'll get plenty of credits and a choice of quarry. You'll also get this.' He picked up the syringe. 'As you may already know, humans pioneered nano-technology but never got round to fully exploring it's potential.' He held up the syringe proudly. 'I had this specially made. I was going to give it to Spawne, but...'

Kira nodded, not wanting to upset him further. 'Okay, I'll do it.'

'Thank you Kira.' He took her right hand and placed it on his lap, palm upwards. 'This will only hurt for a second.' He tenderly drove the needle through the skin in the dead-centre of her palm and then began to slowly push all the "liquid" out until the syringe was empty, speaking as he did. 'You can take Spawne's ship too; I know he'd want you to have it.'

He released her and Kira pulled her hand back, flexing the fingers. Her fingers began to move of their own accord and she grabbed her wrist in panic.

'Relax,' Dylore took a hold of her wrist. 'Let them get accommodated in their new surroundings.'

'Them?'

'Nanoids, Kira. Tiny microscopic beings, far smaller than the eye can see. Right now you have about two hundred trillion in your hand, but don't worry, they're symbiotic. This group is collectively known as The Plunderer's Gauntlet. You'll find it has a variety of uses, from creating skeleton keys and basic weapons, to playing music and recording. It will also hold your zeme.'

At that moment, her hand changed from dark brown to a metallic grey and she moved it around in the light.

'Wow...'

'It will stay like that now. Don't worry, it's non-toxic. Hey, even I don't know all it can do, but it will be a help, I promise.'

Kira smiled, 'when do I start?'

'Soon, very soon.' Dylore showed his gratitude to her with a pat on the back. 'Welcome to the Centuria.'

Patience.

That was the current necessity. In time the location of The Freedom, The Independence, and the key would reveal themselves. She just had to wait.

Gralions were a primitive race but their tough skin and muscular body was exactly what she needed. It had been easy to hunt one down and kill it. The body of the gralion now hung upside-down in her ship. She rained a flurry of blows upon the body, and then lashed out with a fierce kick. Her muscles were aching, but not nearly enough. She had to push herself harder. She would wait and she would grow stronger. She would *never* fail again.

Five seasons later

Although bounty hunting paid well, it wasn't a full-time job and Kira was easily bored. She took to smuggling. Yes, it was illegal and she did feel bad about betraying Dylore, so to ease her guilt she was careful about the shipments she took on. Plus, one advantage of being a member of the Centuria was that she was never boarded or investigated, hence, business was good. Too good in fact. She would occasionally find herself trying to fit the bounty hunting in amongst it.

She knew her latest shipment were chemicals of some sort. No matter, conscience clear. If they tried to use it illegally or dangerously the Centuria would soon find out. Her payment had been agreed beforehand: credits and some zeme.

The shipment was automatically offloaded at the moon base destination and she then went into the main offices to collect her zeme. Just as she was about to leave she heard her name called and turned around to see the manager heading towards her.

Mr Sentan was about a head higher than her and easily three times as wide with a face that looked like it had been melted. Beneath his flawless grey suit, his translucent skin oozed and pulsed with all the innards working beneath the surface.

She stopped and he caught up with her. 'Kira, great job today, thanks.'

'Not a problem.'

'Listen, if you're interested, I've got a *very valuable* shipment for delivery tomorrow.' The way he spoke indicated that it was the sort of shipment the Centuria would not be pleased to see her moving.

Kira shook her head. 'You know I only take on the *basic* stuff.'

He nodded in understanding then continued anyway.

'It's three criminals - long story. I would use another but my best two are being watched by The Centuria. You'll get twice what you got today?'

Kira puffed out her cheeks in contemplation, then exhaled. 'Are these criminals dangerous?'

'Yes, they are,' he sensed her losing interest and grabbed hold of her sleeve, 'but they'll be secured, I promise. You won't have to worry about a thing.'

'Well, it's not the norm, but I'll call you tomorrow, early. How's that?' She retrieved her sleeve.

'Fair enough, thanks. I'd really appreciate this, Kira.'

Kira began walking away, calling behind her as she did. 'I'm not promising anything.'

Back in the ship, Cesar was perched on the co-pilot's seat, checking the navigation systems. Two seasons ago she had got him a gift: a tiny anti-grav unit which fitted on his collar and caused it to "float" on his neck, thereby releasing the pressure on his body.

'Well, we're done here and there's nothing booked for a few days,' he said, checking the log book. 'Whaddya say we head over to Burtonia for a few days?'

Burtonia was a moon that had become a shameful hive of crime and villainy. It was the one place that the Centuria turned a blind eye to because if they went there to make arrests, the entire moon would then be deserted. So, they let the criminals have one final hide-away. Cesar only wanted to go there because he had become friendly with two blue, female pavouk twins on their last trip and now had an urge to go back and finish what Kira had dragged him away from.

'No.' She didn't like it when Cesar bought this up and knew she was in for an argument now.

'Why not? We don't all use zeme to suppress our urges and impulses you know.'

'Not this again...look, there's more to life than procreation you know...what's the rush?'

'Envy is a bad human emotion, Kira.' Cesar slumped down in the seat.

Kira didn't reply. She tried as discreetly as possible to move her right hand up to her neck. There was a brief pin prick and then she relaxed, but Cesar had seen her and snorted smugly.

Kira sighed. 'Let's go home.'

Home was Vomisa 0.1.

Many seasons ago, before even the creation of the Lazis, a Beta Class ship had crashed on an uninhabited planet. The only survivor had been a robot. This robot had no special talents, it was merely a worker. Yet upon surveying the new surroundings it began "creating". First, from the wreckage of the ship it built two more robots. One was equipped with "gathering" commodities such as wood chopping and mining, the other with "trading" abilities. The gatherer went into the forests and collected anything that could be traded, then mined for all the natural minerals that it could. Being robots, they were not capable of greed. They would take trees but ensure that the forest could still continue to grow at a faster rate than they were culling it. The robots ensured that the minerals were not over-mined, leaving enough to enable further crystallisation which in turn would lead to larger deposits for the future. They then set up contact with other planets to begin trading for building materials, construction robots, and supplies. Vomisa 0.1 was born.

Now many, many seasons later, it was a sprawling metropolis that retained a strong equilibrium with the surrounding environment. All power was drawn from the sun and stored in the city. The forests had doubled in size since the cities creation and many creatures that had been looking at extinction were now thriving. The minerals beneath the surface were mined every ten seasons, and then buried again meaning that each time they mined, they reaped the same quantity without having to dig any further and as for the inhabitants, they were not interested in competing with any other planet for power or wealth. The thousands of robotic inhabitants were content with merely living each day to ensure that the city, and one another was running smoothly. They also allowed no other species to live there. Many came offering large amounts of credits to stay in such a shiny new city but the robots would not allow it. They were smart enough to realise that no species would ever be content and it was only a matter of time before they started to want more. Of course, this lead to hostility and some species thought to take the planet by force, underestimating the robots completely. The network of satellites that surrounded the planet were not just for outside contact and communication, if the planet was threatened, they each wielded a devastating shock cannon. If turned to full power, the satellites were able to cut down and shred a Gamma ship with ease.

But Kira was welcome. She had been the first species not to ask to stay or offer anything in return. Obviously, they knew she was a human and what that implied but she was the only one and therefore considered her to be of no threat. Kira had been invited to stay there. It cost her nothing and everything was supplied for her. The terms of tenancy were that she respected the planet and be content with the simple one bedroom apartment.

Kira had no complaints, she was perfectly happy here.

She bought her ship down in the spacious bay by her apartment and then strolled in. There were no locks as there was no crime or threat in the city.

Cesar dashed in ahead of her and made his way into the maze of ducts that ran around the apartment where he had made his home.

Kira headed straight for the bathroom. By far, the thing she loved about Vomisa more than anything was water. No other planet had it in such abundance. When she had been invited, the robots had researched humans and realised their love and need for water. Far, far away from the city was an ocean and the robots had been only too happy to set up pipelines just for her: cleansing and purifying the water while also using the flow and tides for hydro-electricity. Once again setting up a perfect symbiosis with the environment.

Either way, it was welcome and when Kira stripped off and slipped down into the hot water, she groaned aloud with satisfaction. Not bothered about suppressing any emotions. Lying there, allowing the stress and pressure of smuggling to evaporate with the steam, she could only surmise that there had been a shortage of baths on Earth. If everyone had just had a long soak in a tub of hot water whenever they felt angry or uptight, surely there would never have been any wars or conflicts.

Later, having dressed, and feeling much relieved she headed out, calling as she did.

'Cesar? Just going down Bio-Nic for a while…see you later…?'

No answer. She was sure he could hear her; he was just ignoring her because he couldn't control his libido.

Bio-Nic was a bar where many robots spent the evening. They would come in, get some oil on order and then plug themselves into the wall and recharge. Luckily, they also served water. It made a nice change to be able to actually taste something and experience it rather than taking a flavoured multi-vitamin pill or a re-hydration capsule.

Night was only just beginning to draw in so there was a comfortable sized crowd, without being too cramped. She ordered her drink and some poole then made her way over to a side table.

A few robots passed her and said hello. The atmosphere on this planet was always good, there were absolutely no hard-feelings, tension or discourse. The inhabitants had been programmed that way.

Before too long, a robot headed over towards her table. He was wearing a cloak and hood which hid his face from the other robots.

'Isac.' Kira stood up to let him get past and sit down where there was a recharging socket.

'Kira.' He plugged himself in, took a sip of poole and then sat back. 'Cheers.'

Isac was one hundred percent robotic but he was faulty. Unlike the other inhabitants, he had developed a fault in his programming which had given him "options". No other robots had this; they were programmed for a role in Vomisa from creation and spent their lifetime doing just that without complaint. Isac had shunned his role and taken on bounty-hunting and this was how he had met Kira. Isac had also modified himself: adapting and innovating his own design to make himself more proficient. But he insisted on wearing the cloak and hood. He felt uncomfortable amongst his own kind and harboured a strange guilt complex because he could do what they could not. In his mind he was an outcast and a reject, and Kira had long given up on trying to dissuade him.

'So how are things?' he asked.

'Been doing some smuggling for Mr Sentan, he wants me to transport some unsavoury types tomorrow. Good price, but high risk. What do you think?'

Isac pondered this. 'A bounty hunter transporting criminals? What's the problem?'

'The problem is that there's no bounty on their heads and the delivery point *isn't* the Sagittarius. I'm nervous about the reasoning behind this shipment and the possible outcomes.'

'They'll be secured?'

Kira nodded, 'that's been assured.'

Isac put his hands behind his head in an all too human gesture of "worry not". 'You're in a risky business. Keep your head in check, don't stop or draw attention to yourself and you'll be fine. You know, Kira, you've been smuggling for so long now, I'd be amazed if Dylore didn't know.'

'He doesn't. I know that for a fact.' Kira was adamant.

'What do you think he'd do if he found out?' Isac took another sip of poole.

'Probably just tell me not to do it again…it wouldn't be the end of the galaxy.' She took a long gulp of water, and then swilled it around in her mouth before swallowing. 'How're things with you?'

'I've been doing some smuggling for Ryott.'

'What! Are you crazy?' Kira almost choked on the water.

But Isac just shrugged. 'I'm a robot; I'm not getting involved in their petty dispute over who's lying and who isn't.'

Kira clenched her fist at the thought of someone she respected assisting that koontz. She hated Ryott and his rebellion with a deep passion. He had appeared just two seasons ago stating that Dylore was a liar, and that the Centuria were interested in nothing more than money and power. Obviously, by this time the Centuria were the ruling force in the galaxy. They captured and eliminated criminals, helped whoever came to them and actually made the Draven Galaxy a safer and more prosperous place to live. But still Ryott had continued, attacking Centuria ships where he could and continuing to spread anti-Centuria propaganda and slander. Some did agree that they had good arguments, such as the fact that only Dylore, a mere romer, had seen Timm and the entire Centuria structure was thereby based upon his say. A lot of trust was needed. Yet Kira had known Dylore longer than many of them and she had not one single bad word to say against him. She was proud to be a member and didn't take it lightly when someone went against them.

'You shouldn't support those lunatics, Isac. Next time they ask you to help, report them to the Centuria, they're a bunch of troublemakers.'

Isac listened to what she said, but didn't agree. 'Sorry Kira, we're going to agree to disagree on this one.'

113

He was right. Kira accepted that it was better to leave it like that. She liked Isac, they got on well and neither had any interest in changing their opinion, so it was best to let it go.

Isac took another sip of poole before leaning closer to her and lowering his voice slightly. 'There is something I should tell you though, Kira.'

'Go on.'

'Your name is being whispered in the galaxy. Someone is looking for you and words spread. As I said, it's only a whisper, snippets and murmurs, but watch your back, okay?'

'Sure, you know me.'

Isac gave the closest thing to a smile possible for a robot, 'I do, I sure do…'

The next morning as the sun began to stretch out over the city; Kira awoke to be met with a familiar feeling of frustration. Her body was crying out for something and she wasn't able to stop this. Lately, with things to get on with she had taken zeme and let it be. Other times she had explored her body, amazed at how sensitive to the touch her skin had become. Kira found that certain parts of her body elicited incredibly intense feelings when stroked or fondled. She slipped a hand between her thighs where she'd discovered previously that further exploration and pressure in the right places caused sublime feelings to erupt deep inside her that snatched her breath. And the further she went, the stronger they became. Today was no different: the feelings were there and she began to explore. She knew exactly where to press and caress and soon had the waves building up but just as they started to build she wanted a male human with her. Kira knew the way things worked and knew that a male would complete this scene. The impossibility of it made her want to hit something.

'Koontz!'

She sighed and gave herself a shot of zeme to move on.

Later, once she was dressed, she headed into the apartment to find Cesar sitting on the open window sill munching on a Kumquat fruit. There were no bars or balconies, so if he fell that was it. But she had given up trying to remind him of that.

'Morning, Cesar.'

He didn't look round; he just raised a hand to acknowledge her.

'Still not speaking to me?' she asked. She sat down and began pulling on her boots.

Cesar said nothing.

Kira swallowed. 'Look…if you must know, I know what you're going through.' That was the first time she had ever mentioned it to him.

Now he did turn to look at her. 'Really?'

She nodded. 'I have the same urges and impulses, I guess all creatures do.'

'Then let's go to Burtonia!'

'It's not that simple, Cesar.'

'Sure it is.'

Kira finished doing up her boots then walked over to the window and looked out. 'It's alright for you, you can get what you need easily. I'm not..."compatible" with any other species. I'm the last human, yeah?'

Cesar took another bite of the fruit and chewed it slowly before speaking. 'You could watch?'

'You're not funny!'

He slung the rest of the fruit out the window and put his hands up in defence. 'Okay, okay…how about a meta?'

Metas were creatures that were able to take on the shape and form of any other living creature.

Kira shook her head. 'It's an idea, but it's not the same. We'll go to Burtonia sometime and I'll just chill out, take it easy. You can go satisfy your libido.'

Cesar's spread rapidly over his face. 'Alright! Of course, you realise we're going to be there for a few days if that's the case.'

'Enough!' Kira closed her eyes to dispel the image and put her hand up to silence him. 'Make yourself useful and go call Mr Sentan. Tell him we'll take the job.'

Kira couldn't help but feel nervous when she saw the three large cages being wheeled up into the rear of her ship. Each one held a prisoner: wide awake and watching silently. Two of them were identical. Huge, hulking beasts that seemed to consist of nothing but thick reddish-orange

116

hair. The other was of a slighter build but well dressed with long navy-blue hair. His three blank grey eyes darted around, taking in his new environment, clearly looking for an escape.

'*I don't like this...*' Cesar whispered in her ear from his position on her shoulder.

Kira heard him but didn't reply. She was tempted to change her mind too.

'Okay, they're all in and ready to go.' One of the workers patted her on the shoulder, snapping her back to reality. 'All yours.'

'Thanks...' Kira sighed, took one last look at the heavy sliding door that now separated them and headed for the cockpit. Cesar crawled down her back and then went to check that everything was secure.

With a deep breath, Kira cleared herself for departure and then took the ship up and out of the port.

Halfway through the flight, in all truth, she wasn't surprised when she heard Cesar's voice coming over the microphone saying that there was a problem. Deep down she had been expecting it, and made a mental note to stick to smuggling arms, chemicals and intoxicating substances. Things that alone were no threat to anyone.

Kira checked the destination was set in the computer, switched it to auto-pilot and grabbed a blaster before making her way to the rear and unlocking the door, which slid aside with a hiss of air.

Inside, she was pleased to see the two hairy beasts were still contained, but the other one wasn't. How he had escaped the cage she didn't know, but he was now standing with a smug grin on his face holding Cesar by the throat, just below the collar.

Kira aimed the blaster at him. 'Back in the cage.'

'I think not.' He motioned to Cesar as if she hadn't already noticed him.

'You're a bigger target than he is.'

Suddenly the collar bumped against his hand and he looked down at it, prodding it with his other hand, instantly making Cesar gasp and freeze.

'Don't touch that!' Kira said.

He smiled as he began to run a finger over the clasp. 'Let us go…'

'I really, really wouldn't touch that.' Kira warned him again.

'If you let us go, I won't.'

Kira rested the gun down by her side. 'It's not that simple, we don't have the keys. They're at the destination.'

'Too bad for you.'

'Don't!'

Kira saw him unlock the collar, watched it fall to the floor and then dived back out of the room and slammed her hand on the door-lock button, relieved when it slammed shut behind her.

'Koontz!' She stood with her back to the wall, listening to the sounds from inside. There was a lot of banging and crashing, accompanied by some screams of terror from the prisoner. The wall behind her suddenly shook as something heavy was thrown against it and she grimaced.

She then heard the prisoner begin to beg and plead, but it fell on deaf ears and there was another loud crash followed by an unfamiliar "yelp" of pain which could only have been one of the beasts.

Kira had once managed to ask Cesar if it would be worth having the collar sealed on permanently, but he hadn't liked that one bit. He hated it and one day was determined to be able to remove it safely for good.

All she could hear from inside now was a weak, aimless banging noise and figured the worst was over. She made sure to leave her blaster outside and then opened the door.

The three cages had been tossed around like playthings, including the two holding the beasts who now lay still, trembling.

Upon taking a step inside, Cesar turned to face her. He had changed considerably. He now towered over her, a creature of solid muscle. His eyes were filled with rage and in one talon he still held part of the prisoner. He looked at her and roared, showing a mouthful of razor sharp teeth as he swung his thick tail from side to side, bashing one of the cages as he did.

Fortunately, this had happened just one season ago and Kira had used instinct, praying that her plan would work. She did know that time was a good healer, she didn't know how much was needed.

She held open her arms so he could see she was unarmed and began to say his name over and over.

'Cesar…Cesar…Cesar.'

Cesar threw what was in his talon at the wall, where it collided with a sickeningly wet sound that made Kira's stomach turn.

'Cesar…Cesar.'

Cesar snorted at her, then clenched his fists and slammed them both down on the ground, making the floor shake.

Her planned next move was tricky and could end painfully for her if she screwed up. She began to slowly walk towards him, keeping eye contact. '…Cesar…'

He sniffed at the air in front of him and snarled.

Suddenly, Kira leapt at him, placed her right hand on his neck and injected as much zeme as she could, then rolled to one side.

Cesar roared loudly and raised his thick arms upwards. He turned to look for her as she dived behind one of the cages. His eyes now only rage, he picked up the cage with the beast still inside as if it weighed nothing and held it above his head.

Kira was backed up against the wall, counting down in her head and hoping she'd given him enough zeme. If she hadn't, it was going to be messy.

Cesar suddenly shook his head as if distracted and fell down on one knee. He let go of the cage and it hit the ground hard, close to Kira, making her teeth rattle.

Cesar was now on all fours with his eyes closed.

Kira stood up and walked over to him, then began to run her hand up and down his back, avoiding the spikes.

'Cesar…Cesar…its okay now.'

He began to shrink and Kira looked around for the collar. She saw it over by the empty cage and left him momentarily to fetch it.

He was nearly back to normal now. Kira waited till the right moment and then clicked the collar back on. She gently picked him up in her arms, carried him into the cockpit and let him rest on the chair. She switched off the autopilot and continued to the drop off. This was not going to be easy to explain.

'He self-destructed?'

Kira nodded to Mr Sentan and the two workers in front of her as they looked around the inside. The two beasts had been removed and all that was left were the remains of the third prisoner and his cage.

Kira shrugged. 'Yeah, I heard the explosion and ran in to see it like this.'

'Kira, we checked him from head to toe with a fine scan and we picked up nothing.'

'Oh, I don't blame you,' Kira gave them a reassuring smile. 'If someone's determined to kill themselves, they'll always find a way to do it.'

'No Kira, you don't understand. Please, come with me.' Mr Sentan walked away from her and she followed.

Cesar was now stretched out along her shoulders. *'He self-destructed?'* He whispered to her.

Kira turned her head slightly as she continued following Mr Sentan along the corridors. *'It's that or the truth my little pavoukian pal.'*

Cesar quickly understood. *'Actually, it's quite possible he did sneak an explosive device on board. I heard you can get planet-destroying laser beams fitted into your nose now.'*

'Really? You'd be terrified of sneezing.'

'No, they don't tell them. They wait till they've got the sniffles and then send them on a harmless errand to an enemy planet.'

'Sneaky!' Kira couldn't help but smile.

Mr Sentan came to a door, put his hand up to a scanner and waited for it to open.

Inside was a laboratory with about five scientists gathered around the beast's bodies. By the looks of it, they had already started and Kira put a hand over her mouth at the sight of them calmly removing entrails and organs from the now gaping holes in their chests.

'The prisoners were merely a decoy, Kira,' Mr Sentan explained.

They all watched as a scientist carefully removed something small and caked in blood from one of the chests. A high-pitched sobbing filled the room.

'We were using them as transport for these little fellows.'

As another blood-soaked creature was removed, the other was brought over to them wrapped in a blanket

122

which the scientist was using to wipe off some of the blood from around its face.

The creature looked up at them and Kira felt her heart melt. It had big droopy ears, large innocent round eyes and a tiny nose. Its body, although a dark red from the blood, was furry and it was wrapped in four leathery wings

'It's adorable!'

'It's a woebat. They're highly endangered.'

Kira reached out a hand and stroked its head making it purr softly and close its eyes as a contented smile appeared on its face.

'Aw, almost makes me want to trade you in, Cesar.'

Cesar flicked her ear. 'I'm not a pet and you need me to keep you alive in the face of constant danger. You're stuck with me.'

'Ryott will be ever so pleased with these two.' Mr Sentan said.

Kira snatched her hand back making the woebat look around in surprise.

'Ryott?'

'Yes, Ryott personally requested that these three creatures be smuggled past the Centuria...' He then noticed the streak of white in Kira's hair. 'Oh...I'm so sorry Kira...it didn't register.'

Kira took a step back. 'My business with you is done. I would like my credits, or two thirds of them, and the zeme.'

'Kira, listen-'

Kira turned and walked away. 'I'll be in my ship!'

Kira didn't speak to Cesar on the way back home and he could tell she was upset because her hands were trembling.

'I'm sorry Kira. I know I keep screwing things up for you…if I could get rid of this collar, I would…you know that.'

She looked at him and smiled. 'Don't be sorry, I don't blame you…I blame Ryott and that koontz, Sentan. Dylore wants nothing more than to help make the galaxy better, that's all he wants to do and yet there are still people out there, determined to stop him. Why? He's done nothing but good, he's made the galaxy safer, there's less crime. Why would anyone want to rebel against that?' She slammed her fist down hard on the control panel. 'Screw the Rebellion!'

'Take some zeme, Kira.' Cesar suggested.

But Kira shook her head. 'Not yet, I want to feel this for once - I can handle it. The anger is invigorating; it's like a fuel.'

'If you overheat fuel…' Cesar said. 'You get fire and pain. Why do you think Dylore gave you the zeme? You know what emotions did to Earth; don't let them take you over too.'

Kira took a long, deep breath. 'You're right.' She put her right hand to her neck and felt the zeme pump into her, instantly coating the flames, easing her heartbeat and halting the trembling in her hands.

'Feel better?' he asked.

She gave him a contented smile.

Their attention was diverted to one of the screens on the control panel as a message came through.

Attention all Bounty Hunters in the North West Inner.
Quarry: *Rakine.*
Crime: *He has gravely insulted the Dolleu and we want him alive.*
Reward: *250,000 Credits.*
Location: *Possibly one of the old Buena Crystal mines in that sector. Maybe Indor or T'sergia.*
First come. First serve.

'Well?' Cesar asked.

Kira read it through again. 'I've never heard of the Dolleu.'

'Me neither but for that price who cares. It's not like we have anything else planned, and we're close.'

Kira smiled. 'Says they want him alive...maybe I should drop you off first?'

He snorted at her. 'No time...not with that price on his head.'

She began to turn the ship around when there was a video-message on the screen in the wall to her right. It was Dylore and he looked panicked.

'Kira, how are you?'

'I'm alright thanks, you look flustered.'

'There's a quarry that's just come up for a guy called Rakine, have you seen it?'

Cesar was about to reply, but Kira interrupted him. 'We haven't, no.'

'Good. If you do, I want you to ignore it. Rakine is highly dangerous and I don't want you getting hurt.'

'No problem, we're too busy smuggling buena crystals across the galaxy to go after a quarry anyway.' She beamed at him.

He gave her a look of mock disappointment and then vanished.

'You're still going after Rakine aren't you?' Cesar asked.

Kira nodded. 'I'm really intrigued now.'

'So you lied to Dylore - an old friend and the leader of the Centuria?'

'He's just being overprotective. What he doesn't know won't hurt him.'

T'sergia was a forest moon. The trees were in hibernation at the moment, so the vegetation was a mixture of deep red and dirty gold in the sun as they flew over it searching for the mine. The quarry was impossible to miss, cutting a perfect square into the surrounding forests. Countless mines peppered the quarry.

The moment Kira began to take the ship down they were rocked violently by plasma blasts assaulting the undercarriage. Warning lights flashed on the console.

'Koontz, we're late,' Cesar said.

Kira manoeuvred the ship back up out of range and set it down near the edge of quarry.

'You know the drill.' Kira switched off the engine and left her seat.

Cesar switched seats: 'Should do by now.'

Wasting no time, not even pausing to appreciate the warm sunshine, Kira strode over to the edge and peered down. The blasts had stopped but that didn't mean she was any more welcome down there. She turned away from the hole as a grappling-hook formed in her right hand. She slung it as hard as she could into the ground in front of her, waiting for it to stop burrowing and the line to go taut.

Satisfied, she stepped backwards to the very edge of the hole and then jumped backwards and began abseiling down the steep walls.

When she was finally able to see the bottom she paused and looked around. She could see the cave entrance and her attacker: Rosae.

Rosae was a cinsecht. Her two large eyes scanned the quarry while the antennae on her head felt the air for any fluctuations. Her mouth was small and round and filled with small pointy teeth. The two multi-coloured papery wings on her back fluttered every so often in the warm sun.

Kira released the line and dropped down behind a heap of rocks, waiting to see if Rosae had seen her. There was no gunfire.

She put a finger to her ear. *'What can you see?'*

Cesar's voice replied clearly. *'There's two others down there with you...let me guess, Rosae and Honie?'*

Very few Bounty Hunters worked in a pair but these two were twin sisters and damn good at their job.

Suddenly there was gunfire from the top of the quarry. Both Rosae and Kira looked up.

'Kira?' Cesar's voice was in her ear again.

'What is it?'

'Are you at the edge of the quarry or in the centre?'

'The edge...'

The base of the quarry shook as the burning wreckage of an Alpha ship smashed down in the centre and exploded, showering the area with burning, twisted metal. Kira recognised it as Honie's ship; it must have had an auto-pilot, auto-defence, auto kill-anyone-else system.

Kira didn't wait any longer.

With her senses focussed elsewhere - namely the loss of her ship, Rosae was sidetracked and Kira didn't waste an opportunity. She burst out from behind the rocks and ran towards the cinsecht as fast as she could, praying Rosae wouldn't hear her.

She wasn't fast enough. Rosae turned and raised a blaster to point at Kira.

Kira kept running.

Rosae's finger was on the trigger and Kira could see the burst of plasma down the barrel of the gun.

Kira raised her right hand, palm outwards and a shield quickly formed from her fingers.

The plasma blast hit the shield hard but it held. Kira was knocked to the ground. Without hesitating, she took the shield with her other hand and flung it at Rosae. The shield struck the blaster, stealing it from her fingers.

By the time Kira was back on her feet, Rosae was in the air now blaster-less, wings flapping, heading straight for her. Kira stood perfectly still, right hand behind her back as Rosae streaked down towards her. At the final moment Kira swung her now-much-enlarged fist at her, catching her perfectly in the head and sending her crashing into a small heap of rocks to her left. Kira didn't pause to check on her. Bounty hunters were a first come, first shoot, first take the bounty kind.

Kira flexed her hands and absent-mindedly dusted off her chest with both hands as she jogged towards the cave entrance. She ducked inside and kept her back against the wall.

'Okay, where's Honie, Cesar?' she whispered.

'Further inside. She's moving away from you, North-North-West. I don't think she's spotted you yet. No sign of the quarry, but I'll let you know.'

Kira began to make her way through the mine. Like the others it was dark, filled with abandoned mining equipment and many other ways to lacerate yourself. And Kira thought bounty hunting was dangerous. Scaffolding all around her was rusted, derelict and waiting for the slightest excuse to collapse. She could hear small creatures scuttling around in the darkness, running away as soon as approached.

'Kira! Freeze!'

Cesar's voice was in her ear again. She did as instructed.

'She's just ahead, not moving. Look up one-twenty degrees.'

Kira did so and could just make out the shape of a cinsecht against the strictly geometric scaffolding. She could see that Honie was resting with her back against a strut and was watching something. Then Kira saw it too: there was a small fire in the distance. Turning back to Honie, Kira let her right arm fall down by her side. Four lines then dropped down from her fingers and a weight formed at the end of each. She began to spin them around in a circle above her head counting a rhythm in her head before releasing them. The lines flew upwards and upon impact with the strut, wrapped themselves tightly around it, ensnaring Honie as they did.

'Whass zhe-?'

Kira heard Honie cry out briefly and then she was completely enveloped by the line. By which time Kira was already running beneath her, heading for the fire. She rounded a heap of old mining carts and saw her quarry.

Rakine was sitting with his back to her, rubbing his four hands together over the fire. He had a thick head of hair and was dressed in rags.

Kira removed her blaster from its holster.'Don't move, Rakine. I'm a Bounty Hunter.'

He chortled quietly to himself. 'Really? How much am I worth?'

'No more questions. Stand up, turn around, and don't do anything stupid.'

He sighed and did as he was told, and then turned to her. His face was covered in a soft fur that had become matted. Narrow eyes, a mouth full of stained teeth and a face that said he'd had enough of running.

Rakine gazed fixedly to try and make out Kira in the darkness. 'What are you?'

'I said no more questions. Put all your hands out in front of you, wrists together.'

More interested in her than her instructions, he did as he was asked even if it seemed as though he obeyed merely to get a better look.

Kira ignored his looks, she'd had them all her life, and placed her right hand over his wrists as liquid metal began to pour all over them and then solidify binding them together.

'You're a human!' he said, barely noticing that he was now bound.

'Yes…' Kira walked around behind him and began pushing him towards the entrance. 'And before you say it, I've heard it before.'

'I'm sure.' He whispered and then went quiet as they made their way through the cave.

'Cesar?' Kira spoke into the radio. 'Bring the ship down into the quarry; I'm bringing out the…quarry…now.'

Although Cesar was unable to fly the ship on his own, he was able to issue commands and directions that had already been programmed in, such as this one.

'So who's after me?' Rakine asked.

'The Dolleu. Now be quiet.'

That made him laugh and she had to push him forwards. 'The Dolleu, huh? Is that what they're calling themselves now - and they sent a human, how ironic.'

Kira ignored him as they came to the entrance and he looked down to shield his eyes from the sun.

'Sweet, sweet sunshine. Wonder how much of it I'll get to see.'

Cesar landed the ship perfectly and opened the rear ramp as they approached.

She took Rakine straight to the hold and released his wrists. Once he was strapped into a holding device she stood back.

'Okay, we're going to stop off at a port for the night. We'll feed you and then continue the next day.' She pointed to the holding device. 'That can hold an enraged Rhinaut so don't bother trying to escape.'

In truth, he didn't look like he was all that bothered. He seemed very calm and peaceful for someone who may be about to undergo horrific torture followed by a slow agonising death.

'From what I've seen humans are bloodthirsty, but you're going to feed me? What kind of a human are you?' he asked.

'Don't get too excited,' she replied. 'You're wanted alive.'

The Vatera Spaceport was a fat space-station cum hotel where no questions were asked. You arrived, paid your credits and stayed till the next day. While there, your ship could be checked and cleaned, if you wished, or completely ignored. It all depended on what you were carrying.

Cesar said he had seen some pavouks in one of the service ducts so Kira let him go in the hope that he would find some satisfaction while she stayed in the ship, mainly for familiarity but also to keep an eye on Rakine. He was worth a lot of credits and she knew it would take nothing for another Bounty Hunter to still be after him and they wouldn't hesitate to take the ship as well if they couldn't release him from the holding device. Kira wouldn't let anyone take her ship. It represented freedom and that was invaluable.

She grabbed some food pills and went into the hold to see Rakine. He was as she had left him. There were no signs that he had tried to escape, no scratches on his wrists or ankles. His head was hung down but he looked up when she entered and smiled at her.

'Why are you so cheerful?' she asked, perplexed. 'From what I hear, The Dolleu are likely to torture you slowly and then kill you.'

'Actually, I've never heard of The Dolleu before…and neither have you, right?'

Kira shrugged her shoulders. 'True enough, but then I don't know every single gang, family and group in The Draven Galaxy.'

'Of course not...'

She changed the subject and showed him the food pills. 'Open.' Kira dropped them into his mouth and then turned to leave.

'Wait!' He called out to her.

She didn't.

'You're not the last human. I've seen others.'

'Sure you have...goodnight.'

'Please!'

'Come on!' She stopped and turned around, arms folded.

There was a sincere look on his face but Kira still wasn't convinced. 'Let me guess. You tell me where they are, I let you go and fly off to some planet to get eaten by Migronets?'

Rakine shook his head. 'I'm serious, I've seen them. Why do you think everyone's after me?' If able she was sure he would have crossed his hearts for extra sincerity.

Kira sniffed nonchalantly. 'What makes you think I'm interested? I've survived this long without seeing another. It's history as far as I'm concerned.'

'You're lying.' The way he looked straight through her made her shiver. 'All your life you've wanted to meet another like yourself to help you comprehend all those tiny little thoughts and feelings that nobody else can understand. Listen, I'll give you the coordinates, you take us there and upon "delivery" you let me go and never see me again.'

'What's in it for you?' she asked, close to taking a shot of zeme to quell the excitement building up inside her chest.

'Freedom of course. I may not know exactly who The Dolleu really are, but whoever they are, they don't want me for my bubbly personality. I've found something everyone wants and they'll torture me to get it.'

'Which is?'

He shook his head. 'Take me there and find out for yourself.'

Kira stood perfectly still, watching him. If she went through with this she was breaking the unwritten rules of Bounty Hunting and could end up a quarry herself. Yet, if he was right and there really were other humans…well, there was nothing she wanted more in the galaxy.

She walked up to him and formed a thin spike from her right hand. She held the point at his neck making him flinch. 'If you're lying, I'll torture you myself and then hand you over.'

Ignoring the spike, he flashed a grin. 'So, we have a deal?'

Kira retracted the spike, turned around and headed back to the cockpit. She sat down in the pilot's seat and put her feet up on the control console. Knowing she was too excited to sleep, she gave herself a much needed shot of zeme and felt her pulse begin to lessen once again, enabling her to drift off to sleep.

'Wake up, Kira!'

Kira could hear a familiar voice in the distance but ignored it; she was busy talking to Spawne and didn't want to be interrupted.

'Kira...!'

Now her shoulder was being pushed and her ears pulled at. Spawne began to fade away and she opened her eyes to see that she was back in her ship. Rubbing her eyes, she swatted at whatever was around the back of her head.

'Hey!' Cesar cried out as she caught him with her hand and nearly knocked him off the back of the seat.

'Get off my...Cesar, what are you doing?'

He crawled down to stand on her lap and began doing a strange dance on her stomach. 'Last night was fantastic! Oh, yeah! Those two cute little pavouks were the best. An orange one *and* a purple one, I've heard of purple ones and their reputation, if you know what I mean, but never thought I'd get to experience one first hand. They have tongues that can-'

'Cesar!'

He stopped dancing and looked at her.

'Why did you wake me up?'

He pointed back outside the ship, 'those two pavouks? The purple one and -'

'You woke me for that?'

He nodded. 'I thought you'd be pleased. Trust me, I can go for a good season on the action I got last night.'

Kira now had her eyes closed trying hard to fend off the mental images that were threatening to come her way.

'How's Rakine?' she said, desperate to change the subject.

Cesar shrugged. 'Fine, why?'

Kira told him about the conversation they'd had last night.

When she'd finished, Cesar sat down on her thigh. 'You believe him?'

She nodded assuredly. 'Why wouldn't I?'

'Oh, I don't know, perhaps because he's a wanted criminal with a massive price on his head. I say drop him off, take the money and get on with our lives.'

'I can't. I have to know.'

'Please, Kira, this is the oldest trick in the book. We're just keeping him alive long enough for him to formulate a plan.'

'And what if he's telling the truth?' she replied.

'What if he is? There's an old saying you know, "If you go looking, you might not like what you find". Let's say there are humans there. Do you really think you'll be able to just walk up to them, say hello and become good friends? You haven't been raised with humans, you know little about them. You could end up being outcast again, only this time by your own kind.'

Kira sighed and hung her head. 'Yeah, I know…but if he's right and I turn it down, I'll never able to live with the fact that somewhere out there…Yeah, they may not accept me, but at least I'll then *know*.' She held out her palm. 'I'm going. You can come with me or you can stay and play with that purple pavouk?'

137

Cesar looked at her hand, then at the door as he ran his tongue around his lips. He then looked back at her hand briefly before turning back to the door again.

'Cesar...?'

'How about if we-'

Kira coughed and stared him out.

He slapped his hand down on hers. 'Alright, fine, let's go find some humans.'

Rakine was no fool and would only give her coordinates once they had reached the previous set. It was evident that he was taking her the long way too.

Having reached the third set, Kira left the ship on auto to go and see Rakine. He was as cheerful as ever.

'Next set?' she asked, not even coming into the room.

'You don't want to chat for a while?'

'No, I don't want to chat. What are the coordinates?'

'Shame. Very well, the next set is seven-'

'Kira, get up here!' Cesar's voice came over the intercom bristling with urgency.

'Right back...' Kira left Rakine and walked quickly back to the cockpit. 'What is...*oh no!*'

Ahead of them was a Beta class ship with bold red lettering on the side.

'Where did it come from?' Kira's hands flew over the controls and she frantically tried to engage the reverse drive. *'Come on, come on.'*

Suddenly the ship began to vibrate and the power went down. They were caught in a tractor beam.

'Koontz!' Kira slammed her fist down on the controls. 'What does he want?'

'Maybe it's not "what", but "who"?' Cesar replied taking a seat as he realised there was little else he could do.

Kira ran back to the hold.

'Feels like we're stuck in a tractor beam' Rakine said, looking around as the ship continued to vibrate.

'It's the Genesis. What does Annex want with you?' Kira asked.

Rakine continued looking around. 'The same as everyone else. I will miss you Kira, I've got a feeling Annex won't be feeding me.'

'Give me the coordinates!'

Rakine shook his head. 'Sorry Kira, I like you, really, but a deal's a deal.'

The ship shuddered and then everything went silent. Kira knew they were now inside the Genesis.

There was a loud thump on the rear door followed by a voice over the intercom. 'Open the door or we will.'

'Cesar?' Kira called out and was rewarded by the sound of tiny feet running through the duct system, no doubt hiding away. She understood and shut down the hold before releasing the rear door. She took a quick shot of zeme to quell her nerves and then stood waiting as the door slowly lowered to reveal Annex, Tushk and

Damocles waiting patiently outside, surrounded by a handful of his crew.

Annex calmly made his way up the ramp and politely removed his hat upon entering. Tushk wasn't far behind but Damocles scooted up the ramp, passed them all and began nosing around.

Kira stayed focussed on Annex. He hadn't changed one bit and the chains across his chest still throbbed with a soft green light.

'Look at you. Humans grow so damn fast…seems like only yesterday we first met.'

'It hasn't been long enough.' Kira snarled at him, now backed up against a wall but trying desperately not to show how afraid she was.

'Sure hold a grudge though.' Annex smiled at her, displaying his rows of lethal teeth.

'Get off my ship, Annex or I'll tell the Centuria.'

'You're on my ship, human. Be happy to let you off once you hand over whatever it is you're carrying.'

Kira shrugged, 'I'm not carrying anything. I just dropped off my last cargo, sorry.'

Annex looked at her with disappointment. 'Tushk?'

Tushk focussed on her computer and pressed a few buttons. 'There are two other life readings aboard this ship. One is very small, probably some insignificant creature that the human has picked up. The other is far more promising and it is coming from in there.' She pointed a thick hairy finger at the closed doors.

'Open it.' Annex commanded Kira.

Kira stared at him and discreetly formed two claws on her right hand.

'Open the door, human.' Annex said, now with impatience in his many eyes.

Without any warning, Kira leapt at him, claws bared.

Tushk dived to one side but Annex didn't move and Kira was suddenly thrown backwards and pinned up against a wall looking directly into the two mad red eyes of Annex's soul. Its beak was snapping so close to her face that she could feel the rush of air each it time it did and pushed her head as far back against the wall as possible.

'Brave…but irritating. Now, open the door.' Annex was no longer in the mood for pleasantries.

Kira, still avoiding the snapping beak, pointed her finger at the door and unlocked it as Annex retracted his soul and let her fall to the ground.

The door slid open and Damocles was the first in, closely followed by Annex.

Kira had secretly hoped Cesar might have been able to release Rakine and hide him, but she knew how scared Cesar was of Annex.

'Rakine, I believe?' Annex said, walking up to him. 'Going to have some long interesting chats, you and I.'

'I know nothing.'

'We shall see.' Annex turned his back on Rakine and called to his crew who were still waiting outside. 'Take him on board and make him "comfortable". He tries anything? Cut off one of his arms.'

Kira could only stand by helpless as Rakine was taken from her ship, giving her only the slightest of glances as he passed. As she watched him vanish further into the ship's hold, she felt hope go with him and pretended to rub her neck, only to give herself another shot of zeme, hoping it would stop any more tears from welling up in her eyes.

Damocles bounded out of the ship after Rakine, keen to investigate the visitor, and was closely followed by Tushk, calmly strolling out.

Annex was last and looked down at Kira as he passed. 'You're free to go, as promised.' But then, just as he reached the end of the ramp, he turned to her. 'We'll meet again, human. You, I, we have a mutual friend.'

Kira got away from the *Genesis* and headed off as fast as she could in the opposite direction.

Cesar crept down, clearly feeling somewhat sorry for himself.

'Kira?'

She was piloting the ship, but her face was red, her hands were trembling and tears poured down her cheeks.

She sniffed and swallowed. *'No...'*

Cesar made his way up on to the control panel and tried to distract her, but her hands were stuck fast to the controls. She looked through him at the infinite darkness outside.

'Kira, take some zeme.'

Kira sniffed and wiped her face with the back of her hand.

'Kira! KIRA!' Cesar dug his claws into her hands to try and snap her out of it.

He succeeded and she sat back in the chair, hands covering her face as she began to sob.

'I was so close...' She ran her hands back through her hair. 'I don't want to take any more zeme; I want to see some other humans, just to see them, that would be enough. Rakine was telling the truth, I know he was.'

'So, what do we do?'

Kira tried to compose herself but it was like trying to stop a flood with toothpicks. She gave in and let the zeme take care of it then sat back with her eyes closed as the once crashing waves of emotion ebbed.

'We go and see Dylore.' She opened her eyes and with a renewed vigour began punching coordinates in the computer. 'He'll hunt Annex down and send him to Hanaan.'

Cesar rested a hand on hers. 'Kira? I hate to say this but what are you going to tell Dylore? You said you wouldn't go after Rakine.'

'I know...Oh, I'll think of something.' She gave him a glint of a smile. 'Trust me.'

Immediately upon arrival, they were met and escorted to Dylore by two lowly creatures wearing grey robes.

Dylore was currently addressing a small assembly of silver and white robed priests and they waited outside for him to finish.

'Ever noticed how this ship is the opposite of space?' Cesar said, leaning against the side of Kira's head.

'I have no idea what you're talking about.' Kira said, turning and resting against the wall as two silver-robed priests walked past, heads bowed, mouths muttering something incomprehensible.

'It's all white with tiny specks of black here and there. It's a negative.'

'What have you been sniffing?'

'This is supposed to be a place of worship, learning and contemplation, but what do you see when you look around?'

Kira did exactly that and sighed. 'I see peace, purity, and lost beings helped back on to the right path.'

Before Cesar could reply, the assembly adjourned and Dylore was the last out. He saw Kira and smiled then wrapped his arms around her and gave her a welcoming hug.

'You look well, Kira. How can I help? Or is this a social visit?'

Dylore, I'd love it to be a social visit, but I've got trouble.'

He held up one hand to prevent her saying anything else before looking around and ushering her back into the now empty assembly room.

'Sorry about that, but the last thing we need is any shards of negativity or fear floating around.'

Kira nodded and took a seat in one of the chairs. 'Of course.'

'So, what's the problem?'

'Yesterday, I captured a freelance quarry, can't remember her name, I make a point not to get friendly.'

Dylore stood listening.' Very wise, go on.'

'Well, I was on the way to the drop-off point when Annex intercepted me and stole the quarry.'

At the sound of his name, she saw Dylore's hands clench into fists. 'He's been running around free for too long now.' He took a deep breath and turned his attention back to Kira. 'Can you tell me anything about the quarry at all?'

Kira smiled and laughed. 'I'd love to but she was a Meta…or at least I presume it was a she. I captured her by her heat signature, not that it was easy on Carascant with all those pools of lava.'

Dylore knelt down next to her and rested a hand on her shoulder. 'I'm glad you came to me with this, I've been turning a blind eye to Annex and his activities for too long…in truth I was afraid, like most people. Not any more. I'll make it so he can't go anywhere near a civilised planet. Even Burtonia won't want him.'

'He won't like that,' Cesar said.

Dylore affectionately scratched the back of Cesar's neck 'No, he won't.'

Kira stood up to leave when suddenly there was a flurry of activity in the corridor outside and a young silver-robed priest burst in, he was clearly out of breath and his throat pulsated vividly as he spoke. 'Sir, I apologise for the intrusion but the Rebellion is nearby and in attack formation.'

'Maximum power to all shields then.' Dylore was clearly confused as to why he had been bought such trivial information.

'It's not that simple, Sir.' The priest looked at Kira and Cesar as if hoping they would take the hint and leave, clearly not wanting to share his information with them.

Dylore cottoned on to what he was thinking. 'I trust them, tell me the situation.'

'There was a huge theft of buena crystals last night.'

The atmosphere in the room instantly became colder and breathing narrowed.

'Obviously, it was reported as quickly as possible,' the priest continued. 'But it is a coincidence that the Rebellion are here.'

Dylore turned to Kira. 'Take Syjet and get-'

He didn't get to finish. The entire ship rocked violently. Dylore fell forward onto Kira who in turn fell backwards into a chair. The ship quickly regained its posture but klaxons and red warning lights were now blaring crazily all around.

'Evacuate! Evacuate! Evacuate!'

Dylore ran over to an intercom set into the wall. 'Bridge, this is Dylore, status report now!'

'Sir, it was an ion blast. It cut through the Leo as if it were mist, what's left is in Timm's hands now. The Sagittarius took the remainder of the blast and all shields are gone, the main engine's scrap and we're going down on Ikondive. The Rebellion is already taking out our support ships.'

Kira listened intently; Ikondive was a small nearby moon and due to the terrain, not the ideal place to go down in. But options were not forthcoming.

He disconnected contact with the bridge and punched in another set of numbers as the young priest that had first bought the news fled, deciding he was better off seeking salvation than waiting around here.

'Syjet?'

'Dad, I'm scared. What's going on?'

'Don't worry; we're all going to be fine. I want you to go to hangar twenty-five immediately. Kira will get you out of here.'

'Alright, take care Dad, I love you.'

'I love you too sweetheart, now go!'

Dylore cut off the intercom and turned to Kira. 'Get going now, while the Rebellion is distracted with the Beta ships.'

'What about you?'

He now grabbed Kira's arm and physically escorted her from the room. 'I'll be fine; there are plenty of escape-pods. You have to get going!'

147

Kira took the hint and began walking briskly backwards down the corridor. She called back, 'Alright, see you soon,' but he just put up a hand in acknowledgement and disappeared around the corner.

The ship was in utter chaos as believers of all shapes and sizes made a mad dash for an escape pod or spare ship - only for many to be picked off by the waiting rebel ships outside.

Kira made it to her hanger, pleased to see Syjet already waiting, and opened the rear door. 'Get in and hold on to something.' She wasted no time in getting the ship airborne and evacuating the Sagittarius.

Once outside Kira gasped.

War.

She had never seen a battle before; now she was in the thick of one.

'Let's go, quickly.' Cesar said, seeing the masses of Alpha and Beta ships now swarming around the two Gammas. Each and every ship seemed to be emitting blasts of plasma in every colour as they raced around so quickly it was impossible to keep track of any singular ship.

'What's our arms status?' Kira asked.

'No.'

'Cesar?'

'Oh, come on, you cannot be serious!'

'I'm deadly serious.' Kira turned to face him. 'Those...I can't find the word, have just destroyed everything Dylore spent seasons building, for no good reason. The Centuria was hurting nobody; I'm not leaving until I've taken some of them out too.'

'Goodbye cruel galaxy.' Cesar sighed and then bought up the arms list on screen. 'We have ten torpedoes and a few rounds of plasma blasts.'

'Okay…' Kira began to manoeuvre the ship deftly through the raging battle, not made any easier with the fact that her ship was clearly marked as Centurian.

'We've got a tail, Kira.' Cesar said.

Kira bought up the rear display and could see an Alpha rebel fighter, zeroing in. 'Shields.'

'That won't hold them off forever, you know.'

'It'll give me enough time to make them sorry.'

Kira put the ship into a higher gear and began to speed through the war zone, dodging ships with seconds to spare and avoiding as many blasts as she could. The few blasts that got through made the ship tremble, but it held together.

Up ahead, Kira could see a Beta rebel ship. It was stoic, watching from the side and more than likely held someone important to the Rebellion. She shook off the tail with a few well aimed blasts of plasma, making them change their mind, and then turned her attention to the lone ship.

'Cesar, lock onto that ship and on my command give it two torpedoes.'

'Roger, Captain.'

'Knock it off.'

'Sorry.'

Kira sped towards the ship, surprised that it was undefended and seemed to remain oblivious to her ship which was now in a strong attack position with two torpedoes locked on.

'Ready…' Kira sped towards it and then watched as the side of the ship opened up.

'Oh, Koontz!' Cesar and Kira spoke simultaneously.

She pushed down hard on the controls as the blast from the ion cannon scraped across the top of her ship.

'Kira, that blast took out our shield. We're defenceless…'

'Alright, alright.' Kira activated the vector drive and left the battle far behind.

Kira had gone straight to a space-port and left the ship to the tiny robots that were programmed to repair the shield while the three of them relaxed in one of the rest-rooms. The room wasn't busy but there were enough patrons to give it an atmosphere. Many were travellers or tourists, stopping off for the night, a few were freight carriers and there were one or two shady characters in the corners that Kira was sure she had seen before as "wanted".

'Quite a day,' Syjet offered.

'Oh, Kira's always fun to be around,' Cesar replied. 'But you don't seem too down about what's happened?'

Syjet shrugged. 'You know, I appreciated what dad was doing, but I never loved it. As for dad, I know he's okay, I can *feel* it.' She put a hand to her chest. 'He's angry and upset but he'll be okay.'

Kira said nothing; she merely sat looking at the two re-hydration pills in front of her.

Just then a large group came in, clearly in high spirits about something, ordered some intoxicating pills and then took up three tables in the far corner as they continued to celebrate and talk excitedly about their day.

Kira was in no mood to listen to other people celebrating and tried to focus on anything else, but their voices were too loud.

'…We've crushed them now, for sure.'

'Yeah, I'd like to see them try and put those ships back together.'

'That Ion blast was a beauty; did you see it slice straight through that Gamma ship?'

Kira turned her head slightly to listen as she picked up the two pills in her hand and crushed them to powder.

Cesar and Syjet were talking about something and not aware of the group.

But Kira continued to listen intently.

'Where is Ryott anyway?'

'Said he'd come by later, but you know him, all work and no rest.'

'Shame, we couldn't have done it without him….what the? Urk!'

'Kira…?' Cesar suddenly realised that three had become two and looked around. *'Uh oh!'*

Kira had formed her hand into a vice-like grip and was now holding one of the party up in front of her by his throat.

He noticed the white strip in her hair, as did the rest of the group, immediately standing and aiming blasters at Kira.

'Don't be a sore loser.' One of them spoke, a young male.

'It's not over yet!' Kira said through gritted teeth.

But nobody responded, they were all looking past her and watching intently.

'I hate the Centuria....'

Kira was about to turn and see where the voice had come from when something heavy struck her on the back of the head. She left the conscious world with only a distant voice to guide her.

'...And I hate humans, so you're shit out of luck!'

Pain was the first to greet Kira as she awoke. Her head hurt and she groaned aloud to see if she was alone. Nobody answered, so she opened her eyes and looked around. She was in one of the rooms of the space-port. She didn't need to try and recall what had happened; she remembered everything. Wincing at the dull ache in her head, she sat up.

She tried the door: locked. Unperturbed, she placed her palm against the lock and waited. The gauntlet inspected the lock, formed into a key and then unlocked the door.

With a smug grin Kira took her hand back and opened the door.

'Going somewhere?'

She was now in yet another room and sitting calmly in the centre was a casually dressed Ryott.

Ryott was a garetor. Big, muscular and powerful but unlike most species with those traits, garetors were too smart to be used for manual labour. He was in his prime physically and his dark orange skin was leathery with pale yellow streaks. He had thick black hair that was pushed back from his face. His two black eyes concealed little emotion. Two impressive canine teeth, jutted outwards and upwards from his lower jaw, to level with his nostrils.

'I'm leaving.'

Kira went for the door to his left but he quickly stood up and barred her way, needing nothing more than his size.

'You're not going anywhere. I need a favour.'

Kira glared at him for a second, and then realising he was serious, burst into laughter. She went down on one knee in front of him holding her stomach with her left hand.

Suddenly, she leapt up, her right hand now a vicious talon and slashed at Ryott. He took a step back and she missed but followed, trying to hack at him with her claw. 'You destroyed everything Dylore worked for! All he wanted to do was help!' She caught his chest and tore through his top but missed his skin.

Ryott was fast. He grabbed her wrist as it passed his face, twisted her around and then rammed her face first into the wall, hard, forcing the fight from her. With only one hand he held both of hers behind her back, and with the other, kept her head pressed side-on against the wall.

'Listen to me very carefully, human. I despise you and your kind, and would think nothing of smashing your pathetically weak body through this wall. Your life is meaningless to me so don't give me an excuse.'

'Go to Hanaan!' Kira replied, from between pursed lips.

He ignored her. 'I want you to fetch a Bounty for me.'

'Not for all the zeme in the galaxy!'

At that he pulled her head away from the wall only to reintroduce them moments later making her cry out and spit blood.

'One more outburst…just one more.'

'Do…do it yourself,' she replied.

He smiled. 'I would, happily, but I'm not too popular right now.' He paused waiting for a wisecrack but got nothing so continued. 'I want you to bring Rakine to me.'

'Impossible…Annex.'

Ryott nodded in understanding. 'Yes, but I can tell you where he docks. Something neither the Contra nor the Centuria could ever do. Now, do we have a deal or do I have to redecorate this room with you?' He loosened his grip on her head.

Kira tested her jaw. She could feel one tooth rattling around in her cheek. 'What's in it for me?'

'When you bring me Rakine, I'll release Syjet and the pavouk.'

Kira tensed at that and it didn't go unnoticed.

'Yes, the pavouk may not be worth much but if anything happens to Dylore, Syjet will be the most powerful being in the galaxy. She's *valuable* in the right circles. So?'

'I have no choice,' Kira said, defeated.

He released her and took a couple of steps back. 'Of course not, you humans are easy to control; you latch onto things far too quickly.'

Kira spat out the tooth and then looked him in the eyes. 'You know nothing about me.'

Ryott folded his arms and smiled at her. A smug, knowing smile.

Ferraro. Kira had never heard of it. Admittedly, she didn't know each and every moon or planet in the entire galaxy but she had *heard* of most of them during her travels.

She entered the coordinates that Ryott had given her, engaged the vector-drive and sat back as the ship took control and carried her through the galaxy at a speed approaching that of light.

Her feet were now up on the controls and she took a quick shot of zeme. She hadn't liked leaving Syjet and Cesar, yet as much as she hated and loathed Ryott and everything he stood for, she knew he would keep his word and not harm them.

The ship began to slow and then, as if emerging from a long sleep she found herself in orbit above the planet. She couldn't see much as it was hidden by thick clouds that flashed consistently as they pummelled the planet with bolts of lightning. Checking her position, she realised she was on the very edge of the Draven galaxy. Even so, why neither the Contra nor the Centuria had ever thought to look here was a mystery.

Kira took the ship down into the atmosphere and then through the dark clouds, gripping the controls tightly as she was assaulted from all sides by the storm. Once out of the clouds, but still under attack, she got her first look at the planet. All she could see was water, but not still, placid water. An endless torrent of rain battered the ship. Raging oceans surged below with waves so immense and powerful they could easily destroy an Alpha ship. Kira could see very little and had no idea where Annex could possibly dock as there seemed to be no land. But, trusting Ryott, she continued to search.

More than once the violent waters threatened to pluck her from the sky, and through the blistering rain her mind began to play tricks on her as she thought she saw gigantic creatures rise from the waters only to vanish back beneath them again.

At the very same moment she began to toy with the notion that Ryott had sent her here to be devoured by the brutal swells, she saw land. A large island rose high up out of the oceans. The seas continually slammed against it as though it was a blot on the landscape and the moon was determined to see it removed. Nevertheless, the island stood firm. As she grew closer, she could see buildings, lights and a smattering of ships…none of which displayed any Centuria markings.

Then a voice came over the intercom. *'State your business.'*

Kira calmed herself before replying. 'Bounty Hunter.'

There were a few moments of silence before the voice came again. *'Your ship is Centurian.'*

'Yeah, you not 'eard? The Centuria've just been koontzed nicely by the Rebellion. Y' can pick these ships up anywhere now.'

'Land and go about your business.'

"Preciate it.'

Kira swallowed in relief and then smiled at her quick thinking.

She brought the ship down to hover over the others, noticing the Genesis, before landing at the far end where the sounds of the ocean crashing against the cliffs below, diluted the sounds of rapid intoxication coming from the buildings.

She switched off the engine and made her way to the rear door, grabbing a hooded coverall as she did and pulling it on. As she waited for the door to open, she began to pull the hood up over her head and stopped as she caught her reflection in a nearby panel.

The white strip.

She quickly took a step back from the door unsure of what to do. If anyone saw it, there would be no pleasantries. She tried to hide it beneath the hood but it was impossible giving her just one final option. With great reluctance, she bought her right hand up to her fringe as a blade formed from her index finger. It only took one swipe and it was gone, stolen by the wind and snatched from the ship, out into the storm.

Kira had no idea where the voice had come from on her way in, as she saw no sign of any guards or sentries. The twenty or so buildings, varying from one to five storeys high, where set out in a crescent shape, all had lit windows and all seemed highly active. There were a few creatures wandering around against the storm. Many seemed to be just going from building to ship but there were one or two that had clearly taken too many intoxicating-pills and were stumbling around shouting loudly to the storm. Nobody paid any attention to her. She was just another being, head bowed and hidden by the hood, going about her business.

With no need to get intoxicated and pretty sure Annex would be, Kira made her way to the Genesis.

Considering its reputation across the galaxy the Genesis looked somewhat morose and docile standing between two Beta's. The side door was open and one of his crew wandered back and forth. He had removed his top and his scaly turquoise skin glistened from the torrents. But being a hertyf, he was probably more comfortable in the wet than the dry anyway.

Kira kept to the shadows that hugged the hull of the ship and made her way towards him.

By the time he'd realised he wasn't alone, his head was coming to a stop near the door as his body collapsed and Kira wiped the yellow blood off the spike in her right hand using the coverall.

Once she'd taken a brief glance around to ensure she had no spectators, she crept up into the ship. It seemed that not all of Annex's crew were interested in getting intoxicated. Two were hanging around in the corridor ahead. Kira concentrated on her right hand and then slung two slim knives. Both scored direct hits on the heads of one of the crew. As the other realised what was going on and looked around, Kira was already on him, punching him in the chest and then grabbing his jaw as her hand formed a seal around his mouth.

'Don't make a sound and I'll let you live. Understand?'

He clearly wasn't afraid but he also didn't want to die so he just nodded calmly.

Kira took another look around before speaking to him again. *'Where's the Bounty?'*

He shrugged.

She sneered at him. *'Don't play dumb! Rakine?'*

Realising it was useless to try and bluff her, he pointed down the corridor.

Keeping hold of him she pushed him along in front of her. *'Take me there...and don't do anything stupid.'*

As he led her down the corridor and around some corners, she was pleased they didn't come across any more crew members. She could handle herself against one or two when she had the element of surprise but otherwise she wasn't much of a fighter.

At the end of the corridor were four simple holding cells. Three were empty and she pushed the crew member into one, again warning him to be quiet, before she turned to the occupied one.

Rakine was hung by his remaining three arms from two bars, his head was down and there was a pool of pale blue blood beneath him. He looked unconscious.

Kira unlocked the door and went in, quickly freeing him and then cradling him in her arms.

'Hey, Rakine...?' She patted the side of his face. He had been badly beaten and when he opened his eyes he choked and spat blood.

'The human?' he mumbled weakly.

Kira nodded. 'That's right and we're getting out of here.'

Rakine smiled as best as he could and then shook his head. 'I'm not...going anywhere.'

'You'll be fine.' Kira tried to get a hand up under his arms but he protested and she stopped.

'Listen to me Kira, please. You know, when I was younger, I imagined having children, a happy family and being perfectly content, but I was foolish, and threw it all away in pursuit of riches and glory. Only now I realise that all the credits in the galaxy are nothing compared to that kind of happiness.'

Kira swallowed and stroked his hair back. 'I can't lie to you Rakine; you know why I've come to get you.'

He nodded. 'Of course, I knew you weren't interested in saving me, you wanted those coordinates, right?'

Kira felt a pang of guilt in her chest and took a shot of zeme.

'Go to Ido, Kira, there you'll find what you've been searching for.'

'Ido. Okay, now let's go.'

'Where?'

'I need your body to barter for my friends.'

Rakine smiled and then laughed, making him spit out some more blood. 'Nice to be wanted.'

Kira was about to help him to his feet when he suddenly grabbed her arm and squeezed tightly making her wince in pain.

'Listen to me carefully, Kira. Annex has a very powerful friend. He has protection at a high level. I wish I'd never gone to that stupid planet now. This goes further and deeper than I ever wanted to go.'

'Who's his friend?' Kira asked.

But all he could do was mime a few syllables and then fall unconscious.

Clearly, in Ferraro, the sight of two people, one carrying the other through the storm was not uncommon as the two of them aroused no suspicion.

By the time they had returned to the ship, Rakine was no longer breathing. Kira laid him in the hold and then covered his body with a spare coverall before taking the ship up and away.

Back at the space-port, her ship was met personally by Ryott and three other members of the Rebellion.

Once she'd landed, Kira opened the rear door and Ryott came up to meet her.

She pointed inside the hold to the body lying covered on the floor. 'There he is, as agreed.'

Ryott looked at her and then went over to the body, knelt down next to it and flicked back the coverall to check. 'How'd he die?'

Kira shrugged. 'Annex isn't much of a host.'

'Was he dead when you found him?' Ryott left the body and walked back to Kira, eyeing her suspiciously.

She folded her arms and glared back at him. 'Yes, he was. Look, you wanted Rakine, here he is. Keep your side of the bargain.'

Ryott paused, still unsure, before relenting and motioning to two crew members to release the hostages. He then looked back at the body. 'Let's hope Annex didn't get any information out of him.' He spoke with a surprisingly genuine pity.

'Why, what did he know?' Kira asked nonchalantly.

Ryott said nothing and walked out of the ship in silence.

'I'm sorry Kira.' Syjet said, standing behind the pilot's seat as they left the space-port.

'Yeah, me too. I know what it meant to you.' Cesar said from the co-pilots seat. 'Guess it's homeward bound now?'

'Are we out of broadcast range?' Kira asked him.

'Uh...' Cesar climbed up on the control panel and checked the data. 'I think so, why?'

'We're not going home. Not yet.'

'Where are we going?' Syjet asked.

'Ido.'

Cesar smiled. 'Rakine told you the location before he died, didn't he?'

Kira nodded, grinning.

On Ikondive, small one-person pods were opening as creatures dressed in white, grey and silver inspected their new home.

Ikondive was a series of vast mountains and plateaus - on which grew huge forests. The Leo and its inhabitants hadn't survived but the Sagittarius, although no longer able to move was still recognisable. It now sat across two plateaus, the trees crushed beneath it, and a near endless valley below.

Dylore strolled to the edge of the plateau and looked down, then looked back at his ship. He took a deep breath and was silent in thought for a moment. Then he pulled off his outer-layer of robes and made his way towards the ship. This was not over yet.

'We're being followed...?' Cesar said, looking at the control panel.

Kira took her feet off the screen to see that there was a Beta ship not far from them. 'Tell me it's not the Rebellion, please!'

Cesar flicked on the radio and they waited.

'Nothing...' He looked at Kira blankly. 'If it was the Rebellion, they would say something.'

'Here,' Kira stuck the thumb of her right hand in her ear and put the smallest finger to her mouth before motioning for Cesar to locate the Beta ship's radio wave. 'Identify yourself.'

They waited only for the ship to veer away and leave them.

'Who knows.' Kira sat back in the chair. 'Are we nearly there?'

Ido was a beautiful planet. Its sun gave it enough warmth to allow nature to prosper and nature did exactly that with relish. It had no known inhabitants, yet it was home to millions. The lush tropical jungles, vast plains and stunning waterfalls were an enviable sight in an as of yet unspoiled planet of natural beauty.

Once through the atmosphere, they cruised above the landscape as Cesar scanned for life.

'Anything?' Kira asked, watching the planet beneath them intently.

Cesar shook his head. 'There's plenty of life here, but nothing that could be human.'

'Keep looking. There has to be something here. Rakine was too popular for there not to be.'

'Just bear in mind that it might not be what you-'

164

'Cesar, hush.' Kira put a finger to her lips.

'Look at that.' Syjet appeared behind them and pointed to a grassy plain half encircled by a series of waterfalls that crashed down into a river. Stretching across the sky above the plain was a perfect rainbow.

'That is something,' Kira said.

'Hey, I've got something!' Cesar said excitedly as they both turned their attention to see.

'Here,' he pointed to a spot on the map. 'There's a large non-organic mass. It should be on the other side of these waterfalls but the terrains tough so I recommend stopping here and going on foot.'

It was no debate. Kira had already put the ship down and made her way towards the rear door before either of them could think.

'What are you waiting for?' she called back.

The sun warmed the air and the ground beneath them but not too much to make it unpleasant. They didn't speak at all. Syjet and Cesar exchanged the odd glance, but Kira was silent and they let her be.

However, when they came to the clearing, all three of them fell silent.

A ship, larger than an Alpha but smaller than a Beta sat derelict before them. A strange design that none of them had seen before. It had clearly been here some time as nature had begun to claim it as her own, draping vines and foliage over its hull. The ground surrounding it was a mass of short green plants, all with leaves that looked like one of Cesar's paws.

Kira slowly walked forward, transfixed by something, as the other two held back.

'Kira...?' Cesar whispered, still not sure if it was safe.

She ignored him and approached the ship, then formed a blade in her right hand and began to hack away at the vines as if possessed.

Cesar ran up Syjet's back and perched on her shoulder as she slowly walked over. Suddenly, she tripped over something and stumbled forward before finding her feet and looking back.

On the ground was a skeleton. It was still clothed in what remained of a suit and held a piece of coloured fabric tightly in its arms. Its jaw hung open as if in shock and there was a large hole in the skull big enough for Cesar to put a paw through.

They suddenly realised the hacking noise had stopped and looked up to see Kira standing back from the ship, her hands covering her mouth and nose as she wept, now looking at some lettering on the hull

NASA. The Liberty.

'I can't believe it...' Kira said between sobs. 'This is where I came from; it must be a city on Earth or something.' She then looked around to see the skeleton and jogged over. 'What happened here?' She knelt down next to it and ran a finger around the hole in the skull. Then she noticed the fabric in its arms and pulled it free, snapping off one of the arms and making Syjet cringe.

Kira stood up and shook out the material. It was rectangular in shape with a blue patch on one corner, covered in white stars. The rest of it was covered in red and white stripes. Unable to see why it had been guarded so desperately, she tossed it to one side and headed for the side door.

'We'll wait out here.' Syjet called, partly because she wasn't keen on going inside and partly because she knew Kira would prefer to do this alone.

'We could be here a while, best start a camp.' Cesar said.

Syjet agreed and began hunting for rocks as Cesar abandoned her back and began pulling up clumps of the short green plants.

Inside, the ship had not been spared. Nature was the new tenant and woe betide anything that disagreed. A group of tiny creatures ran out, squeaking in annoyance upon Kira's entrance. The first thing she saw were the ten pods set in the wall, all now broken and useless. She had no doubt what they had been used for. There were another two skeletons on the floor here and one in the cockpit, all of which had clearly been dressed smartly for some occasion. She wandered through the ship, taking in every tiny little detail and being constantly surprised at just how primitive they had been when it came to space travel. Imagine using fossil fuels to power such a machine. That had made Kira smile.

In total, there were nine skeletons on the ship. Each one had a large hole in either the chest or head. But that didn't explain what all the fuss had been about. It was clear from the variety of footprints that anything of value had already been removed. And there was nothing of note left on the skeletons.

In one of the store rooms, she found a heap of suitcases that had been rummaged through and sat down to have a look at what was left.

The majority of it was clothing but there was a small leather booklet, filled with photos that Kira picked up and began thumbing through. The photos showed humans of various ages and colours, all were happy, not one single photo showed anyone in any sort of upset or distress and she wondered why it had all gone badly wrong when everybody looked so cheerful. Some photos were shot inside people's houses or gardens and some were taken outside in strange locations such as a large cliff with four faces on it, or a big metal tower that Kira turned over to see the words: "Paris-99".There were also a few photos of a strange four-legged creature that she didn't recognise. The last photo was of two men standing to attention, both smartly dressed in uniforms with three ships behind them, one of which she recognised as this one. She turned it over to read the writing.

"Jake and Josh with The Liberty, The Freedom and The Independence. 3 days before launch. May God be with them."

Kira sat looking at the photo for a few moments and then pocketed it before hunting through the rest of the heap like an animal, grunting and swearing as she threw cases and clothes to one side, hunting. Finding nothing, she rushed to get to her feet, stumbling on some clothing as she did before running out.

The sun was beginning to set now and the sky was a beautiful mix of purples and soft reds.

Syjet and Cesar were sat nearby around a small fire eating handfuls of fruit from a nearby bush.

As Kira walked over, they both looked up and Cesar threw some more handfuls of the plant onto the fire, throwing up a thick white smoke.

'Find anything?' Syjet asked.

Kira took a seat next to her and handed over the photo. 'There're two other ships somewhere.'

Syjet read the writing on the back. 'The Liberty, The Freedom and The Independence. Why is "freedom" used twice?'

'Maybe because freedom is twice as important as independence?' Cesar suggested, poking the fire.

'What *is* that on the fire?' Kira asked, sniffing the air. 'It smells…I don't know.'

Syjet handed back the photo and then produced a small device from her back pocket. She picked up a clump of leaves and scanned them with a blue light.

'Cannabis. Native to the Milky Way,' the device announced. *'Known to produce strange effects in some species but can also be used in medicinal treatment.'*

'Fascinating...' Kira mimicked the tone of the voice and then lay down with her hands behind her head. 'This is… so relaxing.'

Cesar and Syjet just watched her.

'You know, now we have to go and find the other two ships…then we'll have a full set.' She giggled. 'Maybe there'll be some more skeletons there too and we can have a skeleton party. Or what if the ships work? We could fly them around the galaxy, go and see the stars. I want to visit every single star and get a rock from them all. I could keep a display in the ship…you know?' She stopped talking to look at the photo again. 'Wonder which one of these skeletons is Jake? We all look alike underneath so what's the point in having different colour skin? At least with pavouks, each colour is a different type, you know?' She turned to Cesar. 'Right?'

'Without question, Kira.'

'Sure, you know, these two other ships must be out there somewhere. Somewhere in the galaxy right now, there are two other ships. Wonder if they've got people sitting by them with a big fire too. That would be awesome.' She stopped and rested a hand on her stomach. 'Have we got anything to eat? I'm starving.'

Syjet handed her some berries and she hungrily devoured them as she spoke. 'Now we have to find the other two ships, we have to. Tomorrow, bright and early as soon as the sun rises over there,' she pointed to the sky randomly. 'We ransack the ship for anything that might give us a clue as to the location, then go and check on

Dylore, then I really should go see Mum and Dad again, then we…we…we should just…get some…'

As Kira dozed off, Syjet and Cesar exchanged glances and smiles before joining her.

She sat watching the three of them from the bush. The pavouk and the romer were of no interest but the human was. Her fourth command had been to retrieve the key and she knew the human had it, but first she had to ensure that the other two ships were unharmed. Intrigue had brought the human here and disappointment would bid her farewell. Domino had searched the ship herself, vigorously, many times and found nothing to give any clue as to the location of the remaining ships.

Killing the human was out of the question. She would get the key but it was not the current priority. No, the human had to be taught a lesson. She needed to be punished for her interference.

Her hands were gripping the vine so tightly; she felt the skin burst and warm blood seep out from between her clenched fingers.

Yes, for her interference, the human was definitely to be punished. Where it would hurt the most.

In truth, Kira had no idea what her next move was. She was barely concentrating on piloting the ship to Ikondive, her mind was instead focussed on the photo now tucked tightly away in her pocket. Her new favourite possession. She had already spent an age staring at it and reading the text over and over. And she knew, was sure that somewhere in that photo was a clue. She now knew she wasn't the last human, there were others. More like her were possibly living happily on a planet in this very galaxy. But the thought that she might even find her original parents was so intoxicating and powerful that she had to take a shot of zeme just to focus on the now.

'You want me to drive?' Cesar asked. He had been well aware of Kira's far-away look and distant smile since they left and began to fear for his life as they passed through an asteroid field.

Kira shook her head absent-mindedly, still smiling. 'I'm fine, honest…thanks.'

Cesar still wasn't convinced and turned in his seat. 'Hey, Syjet?'

Syjet came into the cockpit and stood between them. 'What's up?'

'You know how to fly this ship?' Cesar asked.

'Cesar!' Kira snapped at him.

Suddenly Syjet reached past Kira and grabbed the controls, yanking them to the left as a fat asteroid sailed closely past.

They all sat in silence for a moment before Kira relented with a sigh and stood up to let Syjet take over. She then took up position behind them, leaning on the back of Cesar's seat.

'Do you reckon they'll all be different colours too? I wonder how many different colours they come in. I should be able to talk to them too. After all, our dialect apparently originates from Earth, so I'll understand what they're saying. What if they're all different ages?'

'Kira, sssh.' Cesar said softly. 'If you think about it too much you'll get yourself all excited and anxious. The last thing you want is to create an image in your head as the reality will probably be nothing like that and your dreams will be dashed. I know it'll hurt, but remember that *something* killed those humans on the Liberty. They were murdered. Humans are not welcome in this galaxy and you need to remember this before you get too attached. Alright?'

Kira closed her eyes and took another shot of zeme. 'Okay, okay, you're right.' She waited for the feelings to pass before resuming control. 'Right, when we get to Ikondive, I don't want Dylore to know anything about Ido, the ships, Ryott or Rakine. Understand?'

Syjet glanced back in confusion. 'Why ever not?'

'It's nothing personal, but Dylore told me not to go after Rakine and although I don't regret it for a moment, I don't want him to know I betrayed him.' She noticed Syjet's look of disappointment and quickly continued. 'Don't worry, I'll tell him everything, honestly…only not yet. Besides, he's got a lot more important things on his mind at the moment, agreed?'

Cesar nodded.

'You want me to lie to dad?' Syjet asked.

'Only if he asks where you've been. Tell him you've been staying with us on Vomisa, it'll give him something less to worry about.'

Syjet swung the ship past a cluster of asteroids and then nodded slowly. 'Okay, I won't say anything.'

Upon breaking through the thin clouds encircling Ikondive, all three were immediately impressed by what they saw.

The Sagittarius now had power and there were priests wandering around gathering supplies and setting up camps. The ship was even checked in as it approached.

'Dad's never been very good at sulking.' Syjet said with a smile. 'He'll have the Centuria back in action by the end of the season.'

They bought the ship down on the edge of the plateau and left by the rear to find Dylore already waiting for them.

Syjet ran into his arms and gave him a hug as he picked her up and spun her around, kissing her.

'Thank Timm you're all okay,' he said, releasing Syjet and opening his arms to give Kira a hug too and then shaking Cesar's paw and scratching the back of his neck.

'Yeah, we took some damage in the battle and retreated back to Vomisa to have it repaired and lay low,' Kira said.

'Good, good.' Dylore nodded

'Thanks Kira, guess I'll see you around.' Syjet said.

'What do you mean?' Dylore asked. 'Everything's fine here. You should stick with Kira for now.'

'But Dad-?'

Dylore shrugged. 'What? I know you weren't happy stuck on the ship; you're too much like your mother. She was never able to stay in one place for very long. A born romer. No, you stick with these two pirates for a while, smuggle some buena crystals, spend some time on Burtonia…' He winked at Cesar and Kira.

'Hey, yeah, Burtonia! Great idea Dylore,' Cesar said.

'He's kidding Cesar,' Kira said dryly.

Dylore gave him an apologetic smile.

'Oh…' Cesar slumped down and sat on Kira's shoulder, dejected.

Skelia never changed. It had been a good two seasons since Kira had last come here but it made no difference. The caves, the pools and the skelms were exactly as they were the last time she had seen them.

She bought the ship down and told Syjet and Cesar to wait in the ship. She didn't intend to take long. Just wanted to say hello in passing.

The skelms knew her ship so there was no need for them to panic or make any fuss. A few waved to her as she crossed the plains on her way to the caves but the rest were content to continue harvesting the poole.

She jogged up the slope to the cave and called inside. 'Mum? Dad? Anyone home? It's your favourite daughter…!'

From out of the darkness, illuminated by the glowing fungus, slithered Forber. 'Hello Kira.'

Kira felt a bit guilty for not including him in her greeting and gave him a smile. 'Hi Forber, how're things?'

Forber shrugged. 'Okay I guess. We've just finished disposing of Mum and Dad's bodies.'

Kira felt her mouth go dry and her throat close up. Forber had never been into humour. 'I don't understand…'

'We never saw her coming; her ship looked like any other trade vessel.' He put his hands together as he spoke in the closest gesture he could manage to mourning. 'She was fast too. Knew where she was going. Straight in, "bang-bang" and straight out again. Ignored me completely.'

'Did you recognise her?' Kira could feel her hands trembling now as emotions built up quickly beneath her skin.

Forber nodded contemplatively. 'Kind of. Of course, it might have been a meta, but why would a meta disguise herself as a human?'

Those five simple letters strung together made Kira gasp and clamp her hand over her mouth before quickly taking a shot of zeme. As the emotions were nullified and Forber began to talk about this seasons poole production, Kira felt completely detached from this planet. Deep down she couldn't deny that she had been feeling this way for a while, just too afraid to admit it. But with her adoptive parents now dead and so much happening in her life that meant more to her than anything, she was no longer a part of Skelia.

'Forber,' she took a step towards him and wrapped her arms around him, surprising him. 'You take care, understand. Make Mum and Dad proud.'

'Uh, sure...' Forber hugged her back almost warily.

She gave him a kiss on his cheek and a smile before letting him go and turning her back for the last time on what she had once called home.

Back in the ship as Kira started the engines and left Skelia far behind, neither Cesar nor Syjet said anything until they were through the atmosphere and could sense that Kira had relaxed. They then came and listened as she told them everything.

'What do you think?' Syjet asked Kira.

Kira took a deep breath and puffed her cheeks out before exhaling sharply. 'Well, we know there's a human out there somewhere because there were too many pods on the ship. But that doesn't explain why they would kill my parents. They had nothing to do with it at all.'

'Maybe it's a warning,' Cesar suggested. 'Someone's trying to tell you to let this go and not follow it through.'

Syjet agreed, nodding vigorously.

Kira looked at the two of them and then put a hand over the pocket on her thigh where the photo was. 'I can't turn back now. I have to know.'

Cesar threw his arms up and walked out of the cockpit, speaking under his breath. *'It was nice knowing you two.'*

Syjet rested a hand on Kira's shoulder. 'You need to sleep Kira. I guarantee Timm will help you if you let him.'

Kira couldn't deny how tired she was and set a course for the nearest space-port.

Sleep did not come easily that night. Kira spent most of the time in a light doze, awaking every so often with the blurred images of a strange obscure dream still playing over in her mind. She decided to give up on the whole sleep plan. She rested her head in her hands and took some deep, calming breaths. zeme was no use. She had learnt from experience that it could do nothing about dreams or sleeplessness.

Suddenly, there was a flash of light at the end of the bed and she was about to instinctively form a weapon in her right hand when she felt a calming influence and looked up.

There, standing at the foot of the bed was a human, but it was unlike any she had ever seen before. It was a male but it was dressed all in white, not unlike a Centurian Priest and yet he seemed to glow all over. His hands were held together on his chest and his face was of peace. The one thing that really grabbed her interest were the beautiful white wings that protruded from his back and gently fluttered every so often.

She was about to speak when the human spoke.

'Go to Tetrona.'

Before Kira could reply, there was another flash of light and she was all alone in the darkness.

She looked around and then patted the side of her face to make sure she hadn't dreamt it. But she knew she hadn't. Somehow a human with wings had teleported into her room and then out again without hurting her or taking anything. She did think that it could have been a meta, only they don't glow. As for Tetrona, she knew it was a planet, but didn't expect to find much there; it was a barren desert, a wasteland. This could have been the same human that killed the others, and her parents, had it not been so unthreatening, so calm. Surely, it would have just killed her instead of sending her across the galaxy.

Kira's head was swimming now and she kicked her legs over the side of the bed just to feel something solid beneath her feet. Even though she knew it could be a trap, Kira now knew where she was going tomorrow.

'A glowing human with wings?' Cesar asked, raising one eyebrow sardonically.

Kira shrugged. 'Hey, I can't explain it any other way.'

'A glowing human with wings told you to go to a desolate, uninhabited planet…and you're going?' he asked again.

'It was a sign from Timm,' Syjet said

They both turned their attention to Syjet and she returned their gaze with absolute certainty.

179

Cesar looked at Kira, then at Syjet and then back at Kira again. 'Okay, great. Just drop me off on Burtonia before you go.'

'Sorry, but you're coming too.'

'Whoa.' Cesar raised his hands in surrender. 'Look Kira, I appreciate what all this means to you, really I do. But it was a glowing human, not a glowing pavouk. Correct?'

'So?'

'So, why do I have to come on this suicide mission?'

'Because...I want you to be there. Think about it: you'll either be able to laugh at me for being so naive or we may find...something amazing.'

Cesar still wasn't convinced and gave Kira a look that enforced this.

'Very well,' Kira relented. 'When we've finished on Tetrona, I promise we'll go to Burtonia. It will be the very next stop.'

He thought about it for no longer than a second and then jumped up into the co-pilots seat and began punching in the coordinates for Tetrona. 'Come on!' He turned to look at the two of them. 'Let's go. Tetrona won't wait forever!'

Tetrona was well described. A barren wasteland, a harsh wilderness and an inhospitable desert. Two suns took turns to burn down ferociously upon the planet eliminating all shade or night. Tetrona was a perpetual heat-infested panorama upon which only ugly red fauna survived thanks to their strong roots that dug far down to gather nutrients from deep streams.

'I hope we've got plenty of re-hydration pills.' Syjet asked as they scouted the planet looking for any signs of life or otherwise.

'Plenty.' Kira replied before leaning over to look at the screens. 'This planet is huge; we could spend a season searching and not find anything.'

'Oh well,' Cesar said. 'We tried. On to Burtonia then?'

'Not so fast.' Kira replied, touching the screen and opening a menu. 'There must be a reason I was told to come here...let's widen the search...'

Suddenly, the scanners picked up something and began "bleeping". They all leaned over to see.

'It's an energy source.' Cesar said. 'And the readings are going off the chart. There's something really powerful up ahead.'

'Great, let's go,' Kira said.

'Could be an ion cannon?' Syjet suggested warily.

But Kira had already taken the controls and was following the "bleep" intently.

The signal was coming from an enormous, circular, domed rock structure that would dwarf most Beta ships.

Kira set the ship down by the side of the rock and switched off the engine, immediately depriving them of all daylight but pleased to find some shade on the planet.

As they wandered around the structure looking for a way in, Syjet pointed down at the sand around their feet.

'Look.'

They all immediately noticed the foot-prints in the sand.

Kira knelt down and traced one of the prints with her finger. She recognised it immediately as it was identical to her own.

'How recent do you think they are?' she asked.

Cesar looked around. 'I'd say they're pretty fresh. Considering the amount of sand and dust that's blown around, prints wouldn't last long.'

Kira stood back up and looked down at the prints. There were about four or five sets and they were all heading straight into the rock wall.

'Interesting...' Kira took a couple of steps towards the wall and then pulled the photo from her pocket and looked at it for a moment. Her suspicion confirmed, she placed it back in her pocket and started to run her hands over the rocky surface.

Cesar took a few steps back and looked up. 'Maybe they've got wings too and the entrance is up there somewhere?'

But Kira ignored him; she knew what she was searching for. There was no question that there were humans here so any lock or opening device would be well used and yet no doubt disguised within the rock. They obviously weren't used to company. Halfway up the wall on the far left, she found what she was looking for as her fingers slipped comfortably into a series of grooves.

'Ah ha...'

There was a discreet murmur as air was released, then a door slid smoothly open and they entered.

Their breath was instantly stolen from them as they looked around the inside. It wasn't a rock structure at all, it had just been blasted with sand and dust for so many years that it appeared natural. It was definitely man-made.

Syjet tapped Kira on the shoulder and motioned to some lettering on the wall.

The Freedom.

The smile that spread across Kira's face was a strong mixture of satisfaction and pure unbridled happiness.

The inside of the ship was completely hollow and seemed to consist of just one immense chamber. Around the edges were pods, identical to the ones in the Liberty but numbering well over two hundred and a lot smaller. Many contained skeletons. The transparent floor was coated in a thin layer of sand and dust, but masses of wires and the occasional blinking light was still visible. The wires ran from the pods to a central computer that sat proudly in the centre of the ship, its many screens displaying scrolling data as it processed information.

Kira was about to approach the computer when something caught her eye to her right. There was a door between two pods that quickly closed when she looked over.

Cesar was about to wander over when Kira stopped him, still keeping her gaze on the door. 'Let them come to us. Okay?'

How did she find The Freedom?

Domino sat in a nearby dune, camouflaged, waiting for them to come back out. She had a sniper-blaster ready and knew it was time this human was taken out. Even though she had lost her parents, she clearly hadn't learnt her lesson or she wouldn't be here.

She was desperate to get inside and see what condition the cargo was in. If anything had happened to them, she would have to be punished again and her wounds had only lately begun to heal from the last time.

Suddenly, above her, engines roared blowing sand everywhere as a Beta ship came down to land.

She noticed the stark red lettering on the side and began to pack up her blaster. She'd return later when they had finished. This was about to get messy.

'Beep, beep?'

The three of them turned to see a young human girl about the same age as Kira but with much paler skin and long red hair, almost the same colour as Syjet's. She was dressed in rags and looked under-nourished.

'Beep?'

Kira's heart was racing. She had never seen another human before and could scarcely believe it. She held out her left hand and began to walk towards her.

The girl looked at Kira's hand suspiciously and then looked as if she was going to break into a run as Kira approached her.

'Beeeep...' Her voice sounded very wary.

'I won't hurt you,' Kira said.

'I don't think she understands you, Kira,' Syjet said as she waited with Cesar by the computer.

'Beep, beep.'

Cesar jumped as the computer began making random beeps and whistles.

The girl focussed intently on the noise coming from the computer though and it quickly became clear what had happened.

'She's been here all her known life,' Syjet said. 'She's never known any other species so the only language she's been able to learn is from the computer.'

'But it's not even a language, it's just random sounds.' Cesar said.

'Not to her. She's been here so long that she's developed some sort of odd understanding with the computer. We can't even imagine having nothing but a computer for guidance and company,' Syjet replied. Her distaste at how a race could abandon their own on a planet such as this was something she kept to herself at this time.

The computer finished making noises and the girl then looked back at Kira who was a mere footstep from her now, hand still held out.

'Blip!'

Kira aped her. 'Blip!'

The girl smiled and took Kira's hand, before tracing the tiny lines on it with her fingers.

Kira was trembling and close to tears.

The girl let go of her hand and then suddenly grabbed her and hugged her.

'Blip! Blip! Blip!'

Kira couldn't hold it in any longer and burst into tears as she wrapped her arms around the girl and held her tightly.

She was so engrossed in her new found friend that she didn't notice other rag-clad humans begin to emerge from their hiding places and wander towards the newcomers.

Cesar climbed up onto Syjet's shoulder as the humans began to touch them and prod them.

They were all about the same age as Kira but there was only one of the same colour skin, a male with a mess of thick black hair upon his head who found great interest in Syjet's bright orange hair.

'Blip...' Syjet said, and instantly received a welcoming hug from the male as Cesar tried hard to get away from two females with short scruffy blonde hair who were trying to touch his collar.

The red-haired girl finished hugging Kira and then held her at arms length, immediately noticing the tears pouring down her cheeks.

'Bleep, blip.'

Kira was unable to reply or do anything but continue to cry. The emotions that were now coursing through her were so beautiful and positive that the last thing she wanted to do was ruin them by taking zeme. With one arm around the girls waist, she stood back to look at the five or six humans that were now inspecting Syjet and Cesar.

Everything was going to be perfect. Kira could see it now. She would take them all out of here, back to Vomisa, feed them, teach them and hopefully in time they would be able to tell her where the Independence was. Then, in time she could start a small colony of humans and…she sighed, it was going to be perfect.

Kira's attention was suddenly taken by the red-haired girl next to her as she let out a long low whistle, and then began fingering the key around Kira's neck with focussed intrigue.

'Here,' Kira undid the chain at the back and let her have it. 'Knock yourself out.'

The girl grabbed the key and then ran away from Kira to the computer, whistling as she did and garnering the interest of the other humans. Syjet and Cesar found themselves to be far less interesting.

They all gathered around the girl and took turns to hold the key and inspect it, each whistling as they did before finally handing it back to the red-haired girl.

Kira wandered over and Cesar jumped from Syjet's shoulder to Kira's.

'Happy now?' he asked, running his claws through her hair affectionately.

'Definitely,' she said, watching the humans. 'Nothing can ruin this now.'

'I take it the apartments going to be busy for the next few seasons?'

Kira smiled. 'Well, I can't leave them here.'

'Maybe I could stay on Burtonia for a bit longer...you know, give you all time to get settled.'

Kira laughed and scratched the back of his neck. 'That's not a bad idea.'

The humans had now spread out around the computer as the red-haired girl knelt down in front of it and fiddled with something beneath the main console. She then inserted the key and turned it.

There was a long low "squeal" from the computer which was mimicked perfectly by the humans as the whole lower section of the computer slowly opened up and a transparent box was revealed which was no bigger than Cesar. It was then ejected from the computer and came to rest on the ground in front of them all, immediately wiping out all power and forcing the computer into silence for the first time as emergency reserve lights came on in the ship.

Inside the box was a small blue ball of energy that glowed, crackled and fizzed inside its prison, instantly grabbing everyone's attention.

'It's beautiful...!' Kira whispered, enraptured by the ball. *'What is it?'*

She was answered by a deafening explosion behind them as the main door was disintegrated inwards. The humans ran to hide as Kira turned to see Annex stroll through the smoke, closely followed by his crew, immediately combing the area and rounding up the humans.

'A Lazis.' Annex ignored Kira and walked right past her to the box, running his hand over it. 'Awesome power source. You humans were good at something after all.'

Kira began to form a weapon in her right hand but was stopped by one of Annex's crew pressing the barrel of a blaster to the back of her head.

Annex turned to face Kira and stood over her, staring her down. 'Had about enough of you. Time you and your kind left Draven for good.'

Kira stared back, anger surging through her at a tremendous rate.

Cesar, having switched to Syjet's shoulder upon seeing Annex, was now with her at gun point. Tushk was waiting obediently by the door and Damocles was running around inspecting the collected humans, occasionally tapping one of them with a talon only to be kicked away by a crew member.

Annex then noticed Cesar and smiled the same way someone smiles when they see a friend they haven't seen for many seasons.

But as he walked over, Cesar didn't share his sentiment and cowered down behind Syjet's head.

'Long time, pavouk. And you're still wearing the collar, so I presume my experiment was a success. Wish I'd got to see you in action.'

Cesar was now peering at him from around the back of Syjet's neck.

'Does it feel good to let go? That was the idea you know. I've given you the ability to release all your

189

inhibitions and bindings. Just take off that collar and you experience a freedom that few others do. Tell me how much you enjoy it!' Annex peered around Syjet's neck to speak directly to Cesar.

Kira was fast. In the time it had taken Annex to walk over to Syjet, she had discreetly formed some very thin blades in her hand and before anyone could stop her, she slung them at Annex.

They struck him in the shoulder and he arched back and cried out in pain. He spun round in fury. The green chains across his chest pulsed violently as he strode over to Kira.

'Don't learn do you?'

Kira stood firm. 'There's plenty more where that came from. Leave this planet; there's nothing here for you.'

'On the contrary.' He motioned to the Lazis.

Kira formed and unformed a variety of weapons in her hands. 'Take it and go.'

Annex looked at her for a moment before darting forward and grabbing her throat. He hoisted her up into the air kicking and gasping as she clawed at his hands. Ignoring her, he turned to the crew members watching Syjet and Cesar. 'Take them to the ship.' He then turned his attention back to Kira. 'As for you, going to let you stick around, lots of entertainment to come.'

Syjet and Cesar were escorted out as the engine of an approaching ship could be heard outside.

Kira began to smirk and laugh even though she was still held tightly by Annex.

He released her slightly. 'What's so funny?'

'I know those engines, you're in serious trouble now.' Kira grinned triumphantly at him. 'Give my regards to Hanaan, won't you?'

Annex said nothing. Instead, he turned Kira around to face the entrance and forced her to her knees.

The entrance quickly became filled with Centurian enforcers. Twenty of them filled out around the entrance and stood guard as Dylore entered.

'Dylore, great timing!' Kira called out.

But Dylore ignored her and spoke directly to Annex. 'Well?'

Annex pointed down to the Lazis. 'As you said it would be. Deal's a deal.'

'Dylore?' Kira couldn't bring herself to raise her voice any higher than a whisper as things began to unravel before her.

Dylore surveyed the scene satisfactorily. 'Excellent. Now I just need to know...' He looked at the group of humans with interest as he spoke.

Annex bent over to whisper in Kira's ear. *'Moments like this make the job worthwhile.'* He pulled her to her feet and turned her to face the humans.

'Kill them all.' Dylore said calmly as he folded his arms and watched.

Kira looked from Dylore to the humans, then back to Dylore. 'No!'

The crew cocked their weapons, spread out and aimed their blasters.

'NO!' Kira screamed uselessly as her voice was suddenly drowned out by the sound of hot plasma rounds being ejected from blasters at rapid speed.

Kira struggled frantically to get away from Annex.

He held her firm, not wanting her to miss a moment.

As the humans fell, Kira instinctively put her right hand to her neck only to feel someone grabbing her wrist and pulling it away.

'Zeme is highly illegal,' Dylore said. He then pressed a certain point on the back of her hand and the remaining zeme capsules were ejected. They clattered to the floor where Annex stamped down on them with a snort of satisfaction.

As Kira doubled up, unable to control the emotions that were now tearing through her, Dylore turned to Annex.

'What do you see?'

Annex looked at the bodies and then at the air above them. 'Fascinating. Look like pale, white, mirror-image versions of each of them. Not doing much, just floating upwards through the ceiling, oblivious.'

Between them, Kira retched and emptied her stomach onto the floor as tears continued to flood from her eyes. She fought desperately for breath between panicked gasps, unable to gain control of the massive surge of emotion that had just struck her.

Annex gave Dylore a quick salute as he picked up the Lazis. 'Pleasure doing business with you.' He then looked down at Kira, still sobbing and shaking uncontrollably between retching. 'What about her?'

Dylore folded his arms as he looked down at her. 'Couldn't have done it without her. But her usefulness is not yet at an end.'

Annex scoffed pitifully at Kira before walking out and clicking his fingers; the signal for his crew to follow.

When the pirates had gone, Dylore crouched down next to Kira and ran his fingers through her hair. 'Don't worry, Kira…we're nearly done.'

Kira could hear him, but was incapable of responding in any way.

Not that it mattered. Dylore produced a syringe and jabbed it in her neck, sending her into darkness.

Kira discovered that she was bound on her back, unable to move. She knew she was inside the Sagittarius by the whiteness and cleanliness, not to mention the two enforcers standing to her right by the only door in the room. Instantly, she began to sob as she recalled and a series of emotional waves pulsed through her. She turned her head to retch over the side of the table, but there was nothing left to bring up and she began to choke on her tears. Without thinking she placed the palm of her right hand against her thigh and willed a shot of zeme. Nothing came except another flood of tears.

As she lay there, the door opened and Dylore entered. He paused and spoke to the two enforcers briefly. They then left, closing the door behind them.

He strolled over to Kira and looked down at her. 'How long have you been awake?'

There were a million things, Kira wanted to say to Dylore at that moment; instead she turned her head to look away, unable to look at him.

'You were the reason I came to Skelia. News travels in the Draven Galaxy and I heard about you from the pilot of a delivery ship. Humans are so fascinating. You have such powerful emotions and yet are incapable of controlling them. Such a contradiction, don't you think?'

Kira sniffed back some tears.

'Be like that then.' Dylore began walking around the table as he spoke. 'But the one thing that really annoys me is why you have souls. No other species is born with such a thing and not even humans are fully aware of their potential. It's as if Timm made you last, realised he'd forgotten to use up all those souls he had hanging around and stuffs them into you humans. Do you even know what your soul is, Kira?'

Kira shook her head, remembering Annex's "soul". 'I don't have a soul.'

Dylore instantly understood. 'Oh Kira, yours is nothing like Annex's. Yours is fascinating. It remembers everything and yet survives when you die. But where does it go? This is what I want to investigate. In a way, you humans are immortal thanks to your soul. You can live forever as the soul can never be destroyed.'

'You've lied to me from the first day we met haven't you?' Kira said.

He took a deep breath. 'I never lied about my wife; she was killed by Annex. But, he's a pirate and I moved on - you don't hate migronets for stinging people. Obviously, with emotions like yours, I don't expect you to understand. I'll confess that Timm never has appeared to me, but even I was shocked by how quickly people bought that, and, take it from me, blind faith is both powerful and easy to manipulate. I thought it would take far longer than it did for the Centuria to reach full power.' Dylore looked down at her in disappointment. 'Spawne was an unfortunate but necessary sacrifice. Without his death, I don't think you would have joined so easily and then, I wouldn't have been able to give you this.' He tapped her gauntlet. 'I forgot to mention it has a homing beacon inside. I've been monitoring you every step of the way. Which reminds me...' He grabbed a small hand-held device shaped like a star from a nearby table and held it over her hand.

There was a low humming noise and then Kira felt her hand grow extremely hot and grimaced. Finally, the device went silent and Dylore pulled it back and watched as all the nanoids fell away from Kira's hand like dust, forming a small heap.

Dylore smiled at her and then blew on the heap, scattering it into the air.

'You're lower than poole,' Kira said between gritted teeth. 'You let your own son die just so you could live forever? Your wife would be ashamed of you!'

Dylore grabbed her jaw and held it tight. 'And you're so innocent? How many times have you taken on Bounty's behind my back? What about all the smuggling, huh? Yes, I know everything you've done. Remember those two woebats you smuggled? I bet they were adorable, right? Really cute and innocent. Well, for your information they're now ten times bigger and loose on one of Burtonia's moons. They've already wiped out six other species, and if they breed...' He released her jaw and calmed himself. 'You see, this is why you humans don't deserve a soul, you think of nobody but yourself. Even when fully-grown you still have the mind of a child and are easily attracted by credits, so much so that you destroyed your own planet over them.' He leant in close to her. *'You destroyed your home for credits!'*

Kira took a deep breath and stared straight back at him. *'You let your own son die for something you can never ever have.'*

For a moment the two of them locked eyes before Dylore broke off. 'Regardless, I'm going to take you apart piece by piece until I find where the soul originates from and then, when I find the Independence...,' he turned back to her with a cruel smile. 'I'm going to have all the souls I could ever want.' Not waiting for a reaction, he ignored her and headed for the door

Without warning, an alarm suddenly went crazy

Dylore grabbed a hand-held communicator from his pocket. 'What is it?...What?...Really...?' He looked at Kira as he spoke and sneered. 'I'll be right there, contain it!'

Within moments, Kira was alone in the room listening to the commotion outside. She heard Dylore cry out, there was some blaster fire and then something heavy slammed against the wall.

The door opened again and Syjet stood there, somewhat dishevelled and holding a blaster in each hand, looking every bit the warrior. She was closely followed by Cesar... minus collar.

Kira smiled weakly and, exhausted, felt her emotions take over, forcing her once again into darkness.

Kira's hand awoke before she did. There was something on her chest and she slowly moved her hand to investigate. The moment she touched it, she smiled.

Cesar was curled up in a ball on her chest, collar once more intact, sleeping peacefully.

Kira relaxed and left her hand on Cesar's back, feeling him breathe softly, and then drifted back to sleep again.

'So, how did we wind up on Persiona?' Kira asked Cesar as he sat by her feet munching on a piece of fruit. The room they were in was painted white with wooden furniture and red trimmings. It was daylight outside and the sun shone brightly through the two open windows. Outside, the sounds of wildlife and distant chiming bells could be heard.

Kira had been awake a while now and Cesar had enjoyed retelling the story of their great escape from Ikondive and the Centuria. He'd taken off his collar, Syjet had stolen two blasters and together they'd torn a swathe through to Kira. The force at which Cesar had thrown Dylore against the wall also ensured that Dylore would not soon forget them. He was still alive, but hurting.

Cesar took another bite of the fruit and then licked the juices from his lips. 'Syjet took one of her father's ships and we made our escape. Of course, it was then that we ran into our new best friend...'

Kira was about to enquire further when there was a knock at the door and Ryott walked in, a smile on his face.

'Kira, our saviour.' Cesar introduced them.

'We've met.' Kira gave Ryott a brief smile. She was still somewhat shaken up about the recent revelations and although she had no reason to hate Ryott, as it turned out they were on the same side, she couldn't befriend him that quickly.

Ryott turned to Cesar. 'I think I saw a couple of purple female pavouks down by one of the lakes. You should go-'

The two of them watched as Cesar, holding the fruit in his teeth, jumped down from the bed and out of the door.

Kira smiled in spite of herself. 'You know a lot about pavouks.'

Ryott nodded and closed the door behind him. 'I know even more about humans.'

Before Kira could say anything, Ryott reached up to his neck and began fiddling. He then took a hold of the lower side of his face and pulled it right back to reveal a brand new one beneath. A human one.

Kira watched open-mouthed as he continued to remove every piece of garetor until there was just a man standing there in a black loose-fit bodysuit. He was easily twice Kira's age but still in great shape with only a dash of grey amongst his short dark hair.

'Feels good to get out of that thing every now and again.'

Kira said nothing; she climbed down off the bed and walked over to him. Then pressed her hand against the side of his face.

'What…?'

He started to speak but she put a finger against his lips, 'sssh,' before resting the side of her head against his chest and smiling at the sound of his steady heart-beat as he rested a hand on the top of her head.

'You're not a meta, are you?' Kira asked, keeping her head where it was.

'Would I wear that thing if I was?' He pointed down to the pile of "garetor". 'No, my names Jake.'

At that Kira looked up at him then fished in her pocket for the now very crumpled photo and handed it to him.

'Well, this brings back some memories. I'd forgotten about the personal effects from the Liberty. Never thought twice about it.' He looked down at her. 'I'm guessing you want to hear all about it?'

Kira nodded, vigorously.

He lead her to the bed and she sat down at one end, grabbing a cushion and holding it against her chest while he made himself comfortable at the other end.

Jake stretched his arms out. 'Where to begin...' Then he smiled, 'of course,' before looking at Kira. 'It all began with your father.'

'You knew my father?'

Jake shook his head. 'I knew of him. That key that you wore around your neck? You wouldn't believe the chaos your father caused in giving it to you. When your father invented the Lazis, the entire world saluted him. It was by far one of the greatest inventions of all time.'

'You mean the blue-sun-thing?' Kira asked.

'That's the last remaining Lazis.'

Kira recalled reading something about that at the academy. 'My dad created a sun? Isn't that pointless, considering the Earth already had one?'

Jake laughed. 'Okay, let me do the talking now...*I* was there.'

Kira relented and let him speak.

He told her of the Lazis and she listened, spellbound.

'Anyway, as the Lazis grew, it became clear that humans were facing extinction,and so many world leaders came together to initiate Project Olympus. Three ships were built: The Liberty, The Freedom and The Independence, with the intention of finding a new home and starting over. The Liberty held nine world leaders; I was the pilot.' He stopped and took a deep breath. 'I was young, still felt obliged to follow orders and obey. I tell you, if I could go back now, I would tell them where to stick their stupid project and stay on earth with my family until the end. But I stayed. The problems began when your father hacked into the system to allow you to leave. In doing so, he screwed with the coordinates, thereby sending the ships off course, in three different directions. When I was finally awoken from cryogenic stabilisation, I managed to bring the adrift ship down and awaken the world leaders. What do they do? They looked at the brand new world they'd arrived in and started planning possible profitability. That was when I did disobey orders. I just couldn't believe what I was hearing. These people had just seen their very homes and families destroyed through greed and yet here they were, in a brand new world, with great opportunities to correct former mistakes and yet they seemed intent on repeating the old ones. There were two guns in the cockpit for emergency use and well…it's all a bit of a blur to be honest. I just remember staggering outside after the President as he crawled away, one hand clutched tightly to that flag - which meant nothing any more. That was the easy part. The hard part was surviving on an alien planet until a ship came and I was able to hitch a ride and leave. I quickly found out just how unpopular humans were and in truth I understood, I felt ashamed to be human. Humans asked for everything they got and I still feel sick when I have to look at my reflection and be reminded of what I am. However, like you I was lucky and the pilot of the ship took sympathy on me and helped me find my feet, taught me about Draven and helped me catch, kill and skin a garetor.' He turned to her with a smile. 'I don't recommend garetor meat by the way…I really don't.'

'Meat?' Kira gave him a confused look. 'I take pills.'

Jake grinned. 'Yeah, of course. Back on Earth, we would think nothing of killing an animal and eating it.'

Kira put her hand to her mouth. 'That's so…savage!'

Jake only half agreed. 'True, but frying bacon and a 12oz barbecue steak…Mmm, my mouth's watering just thinking about it. Anyway, I became a garetor and named myself Ryott. It wasn't long after this that Dylore appeared everywhere giving off all that crap about Timm speaking to him. I knew this was rubbish and paid little attention to it. I was trying to carve a life of some sort here.'

'You don't believe in Timm?' Kira asked.

'Not as such, at least, whatever is out there, I don't believe it has a name. I think it's just a force of some sort.'

'I've seen Timm, he's human,' Kira said, and then told him what she had seen a few nights previous. 'He was the one that told me to go to Tetrona.'

'Fascinating, I'd been meaning to ask how you'd known where the Freedom was. But no, it sounds like you saw an angel. Personally, I thought they were androgynous to earth; I guess not. You're very lucky Kira; the vast majority of people live their whole lives without seeing anything like that.'

Kira didn't feel as honourable as he clearly felt she should and changed the subject. 'So who were those humans in the Freedom?' she asked.

'Getting there...when the Centuria started to grow in power I learnt of Dylore's true intentions through Honie - I believe you've met.'

Kira nodded.

'She's a key member of the Rebellion, that's why I sent her to fetch Rakine too, hoping one of you would find him. I didn't want Dylore to find the Liberty, little did I know about the tracking device in your gauntlet, but hey, what can you do?' Jake cricked his neck and made himself more comfortable. 'Unable to stop Dylore directly without risk of exposing what I really was, I took the Rebellion underground and fought him from there. I kept an eye on you too, you know. Couldn't believe you'd ended up with the skelms. Personally, that was the last place I would think of sending a human child, but I was proved massively wrong. Your adoptive parents did a damn good job. Sorry they were killed, I really am.'

'Thanks, I was told they were killed by a human?' Kira said.

Jake put his hands up to slow her down. 'Yep, getting there, honest. Right, the Freedom. Do you know what ants are?'

Kira shook her head as Jake tried to think of something similar in this galaxy to help explain. 'Ah yes, Migronets?' He noted Kira's look of understanding before continuing. 'Well, you have the leaders and then you have the workers. The humans in the Freedom and the ship itself were meant for just that. On board that ship there's an endless supply of tools and building materials. The humans on board were all unwanted infants when the ship left and it was never meant to be separated from the other ships, hence why they grew up not knowing anything other than computer speak. Syjet told me all about it. She was a surprise too, turning against her own father. Lucky she did, I was ready to kill her.'

'I guess that's what friends are for.' Kira gave him a big smile. 'She and Cesar mean the galaxy to me.'

Jake gave her a warm smile. 'You've done well, your parents would be proud...all of them.'

'Thanks,' Kira half agreed. 'But you started a whole rebellion.'

'I wore a mask. You faced all the prejudice and battled through it without ever once hiding away.'

'I guess so...' she shrugged. 'So, tell me about this other human.'

Jake nodded thoughtfully. 'Domino is one of a kind. She was created in a laboratory. The ultimate soldier. She is strong, trained and skilled. Her mission was to protect the three ships.'

'They sent one girl to protect three ships?' Kira asked in disbelief.

'Oh yes and she's more than capable of doing it. She's almost a robot. She's resourceful, unquestioning and able to complete any task given her. In truth, she's the main reason I became a garetor. I knew she would find the Liberty eventually and it wouldn't take much to see which body was missing. I can fight, but Domino is a true unflinching warrior and she would think nothing of slaughtering me.'

'So why'd she kill my parents?'

Jake smiled uneasily. 'You got too close and interfered with her mission. You're lucky she's such an automaton. Her fourth order was to retrieve the key. If it had been her first, you'd already be dead.'

'But everyone's dead, so surely the mission's over?'

He shook his head. 'Not until the Independence is found.'

'And what's on the Independence?' Kira asked.

Jake smiled and looked up at the ceiling as if recalling a warm memory. 'Everything else…' He then sighed and stood before heading for the door. 'When you're ready, we have lots to do.'

'What do you mean?'

'You want to see Annex and Dylore fall, don't you?'

Kira didn't need to answer. The question was rhetorical.

One of her fingers was broken and blood streamed down her wrist from the cuts in her knuckles. She slammed her fist into the hard rocky wall again regardless.

Where was the Independence?

She ceased punching the wall and rested her head against the surface as beads of sweat dripped from her nose.

In truth, she was terrified. She had no doubt that the Independence would be uncovered in time and she would be the first there. She would protect the ship and complete her final mission. And that was the terrifying part. What would she do when the four missions were complete? She had observed the other human girl during periods, and while *she* would just sit and do nothing, Domino was not permitted to be lazy and such a state of mind had to be punished. Domino had also witnessed the girl talking and socialising with other species; Domino was forbidden from interacting with any being unless it was for the benefit of a mission. She could mimic the girl, try her hand at smuggling and bounty-hunting, were both of those activities not a crime for humans - and she was incapable of committing any crime unless for the benefit of a mission.

She fell to her knees and doubled up as her stomach cramped. Her mind was swarming with unwanted ideas and suggestions and she grabbed her head with both hands and screamed at the top of her voice to try and drown them out.

Finally, exhausted, she lay on her side and began to whisper her missions to herself over and over until she began to relax.

Persiona had not been quite what Kira had expected.

The personans themselves were canine in appearance, all with white fur of varying thickness, covering their bodies. Like the Centurians, there were three types of personans: The young ones that had yet to earn a soul and

206

wore simple hand-made white gowns. The older ones, ready to receive a soul wore the same gowns, but with red or gold stitching depending on their abilities. While the elders wore beautiful gowns, intricately decorated with stunning embroidery.

Persiona itself was a tapestry of endless fields and high foreboding mountains - where the younger personans went to meditate. The settlement they were currently in was situated on a plateau near the base of one such mountain. Endless plains stretched out from the base with the odd lake dotted here and there.

A personan's entire life was dedicated to receiving a soul. Nothing else mattered. They had no ships and little technology; content to live in harmony with their planet and having no desire to travel or make contact with other races.

Kira had been loved in her life. She had been adored, cared for, liked and even hated, but she had never been worshipped before. Until now.

The personans could not do enough for her and Jake. No matter what they requested, it was brought one way or another, and their every move was watched in case they needed something. Syjet and Cesar were also looked after, but not to the same extent.

It wasn't till later that day, when Kira was lying on the grass next to Jake watching a flock of quad-winged birds fly overhead, that she finally decided to ask what was going on.

Jake laughed. 'Takes some getting used to, doesn't it?' He then rolled over onto his side to face her. 'They worship us because they spend their entire lives trying to earn the right to host a soul; we're born with one.'

Kira felt her muscles tense at an unwelcome memory. 'I don't have a soul!'

He rested a comforting hand on her shoulder. 'Relax, ours are nothing like Annex's.'

But Kira wasn't convinced. 'So, where is it? Surely I would have seen it by now or felt it?'

Jake scoffed in gentle scorn. 'Kira, the human race spent its entire existence asking that very same question and yet nobody doubted that we had one. Just because you can't see it, doesn't mean it isn't there. This is why the persionans worship us, because they can sense it.'

'Well, what does it do?' Kira asked, chewing on a piece of grass.

Jake puffed out his cheeks and lay on his back again with one hand under his head. 'I'm just a pilot that became a garetor and started a revolution, how would I know? All I know is that we do have one.'

'Maybe it's like the appendix?' Kira asked. 'You know, its there, but you don't really need it.'

He smiled. 'No, I think it's more like our minds. We only know how to use ten percent of it, so there's a lot of potential for us humans.'

Kira moved so she was resting her head on his chest and lay back to watch a cloud drift by. 'Why did humans destroy themselves when they had so much great stuff in their life?' She asked contemplatively. 'They had souls, music, baths and a planet that had every type of terrain and scenery you could wish for.'

Jake stroked her head affectionately. 'Because money… sorry, credits were more important to them.'

Kira shrugged. 'Well, sure its fun to have some credits, but they didn't have to pay to live on Earth did they?'

'It depended how much of Earth you wanted.'

'Crazy…'

'You're your father's daughter alright,' he said. 'Those are the exact same ideas he had. You know, theoretically, he's watching over you right now.'

'How?' Kira asked, spitting out the grass and wiping the bitter sap from her lips.

'Well, as you saw at the Freedom, when a human dies, the soul doesn't, it's released. The theory was that all souls went to a place called heaven and stayed there until it was time for them to return in a new body.'

Kira turned her head to look at him with distaste on her face. 'You mean I have someone else's soul inside me?'

Jake shook his head and blew his fringe out of his face. 'I don't know much more than you to be honest. Sorry.'

'That's alright; it's just nice to finally be with someone I can relate to.'

The two of them watched Syjet swimming and relaxing in the lake at the bottom of the hill while Cesar did his best to impress two purple pavouks.

'Kira, can I ask you something personal?' Jake asked.

Kira shrugged. 'Sure.'

'Have you ever had sex?'

Kira shook her head. 'Not exactly...not really, no...I mean I've read about it and stuff, but never actually...' She stopped and stared at him. 'Have you?'

He nodded. 'But not for some time now...'

Later that evening, as the sun bathed the distant hills and sky in a fierce red, Kira took a deep breath and pressed her face to Jake's neck as she wound her fingers around the dark hairs on his chest.

He kissed the top of her head and pushed his hair back, exhaling calmly from his nostrils before wrapping his arms around her.

Kira felt as if someone had just released a pressure valve deep within her. She could feel her entire body glowing and with each breath mewed softly.

That was good...' she said. *'I can see why Cesar makes such a fuss about it.'*

Jake agreed. 'Thanks to our emotions, humans have far better sex lives than any other species. I've seen much of this galaxy and the vast majority of its inhabitants, excepting pavouks and a few others, see sex merely as a form of procreation. With us, it's far more than just physical, it can be so deep and-'

Kira stopped him with a finger to his lips. *'I understand...'*

The following morning when Kira awoke, she felt as if a huge swelling had been removed. Whatever it was that had been building up inside her had vanished and she felt a wonderful sense of peace and tranquillity within.

She was alone in the bed but rolled over onto her side to watch Jake dress. She let her eyes linger over the muscles in his back and arms and smiled to herself as she recalled last night. Recalled, with pleasure, exploring every last inch of his body with her fingers and the way he had done the same to her.

Dressed, he turned back to the bed and leant over to give her a good morning kiss. 'When you're ready, we have a lot to do.'

'Such as?' Kira asked, holding his face for another kiss.

'You'll see.'

Once Kira was ready, she made her way outside into the courtyard where she was met by Cesar, jumping onto her shoulder as she passed him.

'I vote we stay here.' he said, munching on a blue cubic piece of fruit.

'We're not finished yet, my little pavoukian pal.'

'You looked pretty finished last night...at long last, eh?' he elbowed her ear.

She stopped walking and tried to look around at him. 'You didn't watch, did you?'

'Not for long, ewww.' Cesar spat out a pip. 'Watching you humans getting all sappy and drooling over each other is enough to put any species off their food, besides, I had two purple pavouks to entertain.'

'Still want to go to Burtonia?'

'Not just yet.' he gave her a massive grin, displaying his juice-stained teeth, before leaping off her shoulder, and running away.

Kira watched him go and then raised her arms above her head and stretched, taking a deep breath as she did and sighing in the sunlight.

'Miss Kira?'

She turned to see two persionans standing behind her; hands clasped together, heads bowed.

'Yes?'

'The Elder Council wishes to meet with you.'

Well, I hadn't made any other plans, so…'

They nodded in understanding. 'We will escort you.'

The Elder Council did not meet in an immense hall and they did not actually consider themselves as any sort of leaders. But the fourteen of them were the only persionans to receive souls.

They were sat spread out in a circle beneath a simple wooden construct with a domed roof, covered in foliage. Small bells and chimes hung down from the roof above their heads "singing" each time a breeze passed.

As Kira came into the circle and stood in the centre, they each bowed their head to her in respect.

'Kira.' The eldest persionan pulled himself up onto his walking stick and took a few steps towards her. 'What do you fear?'

'I fear nothing,' she replied.

He shook his head. 'You fear Annex and you fear his soul. I suspect you still have nightmares where you see that green bird rise up above you, its eyes red with fury. Correct?'

Kira nodded, trying to disguise the fact that she was trembling.

The elder rested a hand on her chest and closed his eyes. 'Yes...your soul is ready. For most of your life, it has been a mere spectator. No longer, understand?'

'But I-'

'Your soul is twice as powerful as Annex's. If you believe in your soul and the power you possess, Annex will fall before you. His soul wants nothing more than freedom; it serves him only in the hope that he will one day release it. Yours is like a brother to you, it wants to help. Believe, Kira. Believe.'

At that, the remaining council members stood up and then opened their arms.

Kira gasped.

From each of them rose a golden spirit. All were different, some resembled creatures Kira had never seen and one even closely resembled a skelm. But all thirteen souls stared at her with respect and their pure white, glowing eyes filled her with strength as the elder took his hand from her chest and looked her in the eyes too.

'Well, Kira?'

Kira looked down at him, then at the thirteen golden souls around her and finally, past them all, over the plains to the horizon. 'I believe.'

The council said nothing as their souls were once again drawn back inside them. They then sat down and the elder gave one final bow to Kira before slowly returning to his seat.

Kira was about to say something, when she saw Syjet standing just outside the structure, leaning against a rock. Her hair was tied back and her face was marked with black paint. On each thigh she had a blaster and across her chest were a string of grenades.

Kira gave one final bow to the council and then left the construct to see her.

Syjet said nothing; she just motioned for Kira to follow her around the corner along a low plateau.

'Where are you going dressed like that, young lady?' Kira asked.

Syjet patted the blasters on her thighs. 'We've got an appointment with Annex. Want to come?'

Before Kira could answer, they walked around one side of the mountain to be met by an immense plateau and a series of caves. Thirty Alpha ships and ten Beta ships hovered and darted around in the air as the Rebellion prepared for war. There were easily over a hundred members, all climbing into ships or taking as many weapons as they could carry.

'You realise who'll be next don't you Syjet?'

Syjet stood watching the preparations. 'I know, and I feel no pity for him. He let my brother die and sided with the monster that killed my mother.' She turned to Kira. 'I may not have the strong emotions you have, but I don't forgive that easily and besides,' she rested a hand on Kira's back and began pushing her towards the activity, 'he threatened a good friend of mine.'

'Kira!'

They both turned to their left to see Jake make his way beneath one of the ships, now back in his garetor costume.

'I'll leave you two be.' Syjet gave Kira a wink and then jogged off, calling back as she went. 'See you on the Genesis!'

Kira watched her go and then turned to Jake with disappointment in her eyes at his outfit.

He noticed and rested a large hand on the back of her head. 'It's not like that, Kira. Domino is still alive somewhere and she wants me dead. The last thing we need is her complicating this mission.'

Kira nodded in understanding. 'What exactly is the mission?'

'We have to retrieve the Lazis. The Independence will be useless without it...not to mention, putting a stop to Annex for good.' He moved his arm to rest around her shoulder and took her hands. 'Did the council give you the lecture about your soul?'

'Yeah, and massively confused me at the same time.'

He smiled and shook his head. 'It's easy, just have faith in it. Believe in yourself and the fact that you are more powerful than Annex could ever hope to be.'

Kira gave a lop-sided smile. 'Okay…but I think its going to take more than a soul to stop Annex, if you know what I mean…'

With a brief chortle he took her hand and lead her to one of the caves. 'Of course, the soul is best used in defence. What you need is a tomahawk.'

In one corner stood a lone table with a bright light above it. Whatever was on it, was nearly the same size as Kira and covered in a cloth.

'Abracadabra.' Jake pulled the cloth away to reveal a cannon. It looked as if it had been removed from some sort of warship and was silver in colour with lights and sensors dotted around the barrel. There was a clear dome in the centre, above the triggers that housed a cluster of buena crystals.

'What do you think?' he asked.

'It looks pretty damn awesome…' she replied, running her hand along the massive barrel. 'Shame I'm not a garetor.' She flexed her arm muscles at him with a shrug.

But he stood firm. 'Try it.'

Unsure, Kira leant over the table with both hands and prepared herself to take the strain, only to find it almost floated off the table.

'It's fitted with three anti-grav devices,' Jake said. 'It'll still be a bit unwieldy but it'll put a hole through an Alpha class with ease.'

She picked it up and manoeuvred it until she felt comfortable with it before slinging the strap over her shoulder and aiming it around the cave. 'Feel the need to test it...' She said, looking around for a harmless target.

But Jake stepped in and put a hand over the barrel aiming it down at the ground. 'You'll get plenty of practice later. Until then, just trust me that it does work.'

Kira placed it back on the table and then took a step towards Jake and wrapped both arms around his neck before kissing his cheek. *Thank you.*

Tauria.

She had been coming to Tauria for a while now. It was a solitary city on one of Burtonia's moons. Due to the lethal gases that made up the atmosphere, the city was housed inside an immense dome, therefore bathing the city in the constant red-glow from the volatile weather outside.

But the real reason she liked Tauria was that it was easy to become lost here. Everyone here had some sort of secret or past that they were trying to hide from and therefore you didn't have to go far to find an intoxication bar and then immerse yourself in a dark corner to be alone and uninterrupted with your thoughts.

She took a seat in a far corner, almost completely enshrouded by shadow and ordered a handful of pills from a nearby robot. She then rested her elbows on the table and cradled her head in her hands as she stared at a stain on the table. But before she could let her mind wander over recent events and her uncertain future, a small hover-bot flew over her table dropping an advertising leaflet as it did before doing the same at the table behind.

She glanced at it and saw that it was an advert for Burtonia. She didn't need to read any more, she knew of that planet and had no interest in it. From what she'd heard, there was nothing that couldn't be found or experienced on Burtonia, no matter how depraved or foul your tastes were. It was of no use to her. Her mind was focussed on the missions and nothing more. The last thing she needed was a distraction or to lose sight of her objectives.

She picked up the leaflet and was about to start tearing it into tiny pieces, when something caught her eye and she gripped the leaflet tightly as she read it through.

When the robot returned with her pills, she was already gone.

To Kira's surprise, only two Beta ships and two Alpha ships actually left Persiona, even if they were packed with heavily-armed members of the Rebellion. She took a seat amongst them and rested the tomahawk on the floor next to her, immediately receiving a few nods and glances of admiration from those around her. She didn't know where Syjet was but she could see Jake, or Ryott as he currently was, standing just outside the cockpit conversing with the pilot. He gave her a brief wink and then turned his attention to a younger member to his left who was having trouble with his blaster.

Kira was about to sit back and relax when something dropped down onto her lap from the weapon racks above, making her jump.

'Not too late am I?' Cesar perched on her knee.

She took a deep breath and waited for her heart to return to its usual position as she eyed him with mock irritation.

'You look tense,' he rubbed her knee to try and reassure her. 'You sure you want to do this? We don't mind if you stay behind and let the warriors take care of this, right people?' He looked around at the members that were now watching him and received a few cheers, whistles and some clapping.

'What are you going to do, hump their legs?' Kira asked, arms now folded.

He looked at her and snarled, baring his teeth. 'Nope, when I take off this here collar,' he patted it confidently. 'I'm going to kick so much pirate rear-end, you guys are going to be left taking pot-shots at each other just to alleviate the boredom. In fact, you might as well just drop me off, go and turn the ship around then pick me up on the way back. No need for all this hardware with Cesar on board.' He pointed to the tomahawk mockingly as he received a few more cheers.

'So, you had fun with those purple pavouks I take it?' Kira asked.

Cesar just smiled at her as he lay down on her lap, hands behind his head. 'I tell you, I am the lord of all I survey.'

'Well, I wager I take out more pirates than you do.' She poked a finger in his stomach as the surrounding members egged them on with cheers.

'Deal.' Cesar sat up. 'If I win, we spend two seasons on Burtonia.'

Kira grimaced. 'Alright, but if I win, you don't even mention Burtonia for three seasons.'

'Deal.' They shook hands as more cheering erupted around them.

'ALERT, ALERT!'

Everyone fell silent as they were bathed in red light.

'The Genesis is dead ahead, so let's get our shit together,' Ryott spoke over the intercom. 'We're only going to get one shot at this...and they know we're coming.'

As if to prove his point, there was a loud crash and the ship jerked violently to the right as a plasma blast struck the shields.

They all watched in silence as the two Alpha ships took out the side cannons and paved the way for them to dock. In no time, the two Beta ships had initiated docking procedures and were cutting through the Genesis' airlocks.

'Cesar, time to do your thing.' Ryott called, summoning him.

'Hey...' Kira went to protest as Cesar jumped down off her lap.

He turned and spoke to everyone smugly. 'Oh, I forgot to mention, I'm the "secret-weapon". It's my job to go in and take out the first waves.' He turned to Kira and winked. 'Burtonia, here I come!'

As Cesar strolled smugly towards the airlock, one of the other members turned to Kira. 'Bad luck, but don't worry, I hear Burtonia's great during the next two seasons.'

'I'm not worried,' Kira shrugged, then sat back with her hands behind her head. 'I'm the "super-secret weapon", it's my job to take out Annex himself. A fifty point bonus I do believe?'

The time for laughter and jokes came to an end as everyone began filing towards the airlocks, making last-minute adjustments to weapons and giving each other remarks of support as they did.

Kira was last, as ordered/ At the airlock, she was stopped by Ryott; the sounds of intense battle unmistakable from inside.

'Here,' he handed her Cesar's collar. 'He's finally gaining control of it. Annex created his own worst enemy.'

'You're not coming?' she asked.

He smiled and shook his head. 'There's no need for me to go too. I don't doubt for a second that they'll succeed and I want to be here when they do. Besides, do you have any idea how slow it is moving around in this thing.' He motioned down to his costume.

221

'Coward.' She gave him a cheeky grin as he adjusted her titanius-vest, making her wince.

He moved his arm to let her go. 'Okay, just remember-'

But before he could finish, she stood on tiptoes and kissed his cheek. 'Yeah, yeah, I know, *believe!*'

She didn't bother to say goodbye, she just strolled towards the airlock, tomahawk at her side and entered the Genesis.

Although she had missed the best part of the battle, it was far from over. Annex had a large crew and not one of them was the surrendering type. Immediately upon entering, she heard a cry to her left and one of the pirates charged at her with an electro-mace. She aimed the tomahawk, pulled the trigger and took a step back as a bright green blast of plasma, tore straight through him and slammed into the wall behind him. What was left collapsed to the floor in a smouldering heap and she whistled her approval before moving further inside.

The battle was still raging in the distance and she was pleased to see that most of the bodies had once been pirates. The walls were a mass of plasma blasts, blood and claw marks, which she instantly recognised. Around the next corner, she came into the heart of the ship, an immense chamber that was clearly used for a variety of purposes. Not only were there skeletons of poor hapless victims still manacled to the walls, but beneath them sat crates and containers, no doubt holding goods that had not been bought with credits. There were tables in the centre, many of which were now either burning, overturned or in splinters.

Another member of the rebellion saw her and waved as he stopped peering through the containers. She didn't get a chance to wave back. There was a scuttling sound and Damocles leapt onto his face and began hacking at him with his talons and simultaneously squeezing the life from him with his tentacles.

Kira raised her gun to aim at him, but he was too small a target.

As the member collapsed to the floor with little remaining of his head, Damocles saw her and his eye widened. He began scuttling towards her, easily dodging her blasts before jumping up onto the barrel of the gun. She tried to shake him off but he just flexed his talons and leapt at her head. Kira ducked down and slipped on the remains of a pirate, falling onto her back. Damocles landed on her chest and quickly wrapped a tentacle around her neck. He began to squeeze as he reached for her face with his blood-stained talons.

Kira tried desperately to remove the tentacle from her neck with one hand while fighting off the talons with her other. Her air supply was dwindling and she felt herself wanting to sleep. Her eyes began to close and her swipes lost their strength.

The ground shook as something big and heavy strolled over.

There was a sickening wet noise and she was splattered with something warm as the tentacle around her neck fell limp. She rolled over onto all fours, with her hand to her throat, to try and regain her breath. When she opened her eyes she was met by two hefty, yellow, scaled feet and looked up to see Cesar looking down at her. He had clearly seen his fair share of action. His body was covered in scratches and bruises and both his paws were dripping with various bodily fluids, from various species.

Kira slowly stood up and rested a hand on his chest as he continued to stare at her, not speaking.

'Cesar?' she asked softly.

He bared his teeth at her briefly, then snorted and growled in the back of his throat. Kira took a cautious step away from him. He didn't attack, he just lowered his head and pushed at her. Kira smiled and patted him on the back of the head. 'Good work my little...big pavoukian pal, good work.'

Cesar stood back up and thumped his chest once with his fist then picked up the tomahawk and handed it to her.

She took it and slung it over her shoulder then pointed in the direction of the ship. 'Cesar, go back to the ship.'

He snorted once more and then lumbered off.

Kira dusted herself down and smiled to herself before jogging across the hallway to the stairway at the other end. At the top of the stairs was a long corridor that turned a corner. She followed the corridor, tomahawk ready. The silence, the bodies on the floor and the blast marks on the walls assured her that this area had already seen the worst part of the battle. In the far distance she could still hear fighting, but the nearby area was silent. When she turned the corner, she saw why: five rebellion members were stood outside a sealed door that clearly lead to the bridge and Annex, but she knew as well as them that they had been given strict instructions to leave Annex to her. So, they were doing just that. Explosives had already been set on the door and the members stood back as Kira approached, stepping over a body as she did that she was pretty sure had once been Tushk.

The member nearest the door, holding the detonator in his hand, gave her an okay symbol and she mimicked it then turned her head like everyone else as the explosives went off, deafening them all temporarily. As the door was blown inwards, Kira suddenly found herself alone as the members turned and ran past her, leaving her to fulfil her own personal mission.

With the tomahawk in front of her and her finger on the trigger, she stepped through the smoke and charred metal into the bridge.

It was a triangular shape. She was currently at the point of the triangle, there was a short walkway, where the door now lay, and then a series of stairs that widened out onto the main control deck, where a series of consoles bleeped and flashed. The pitch black, star-speckled sky was visible through the row of windows.

'You?' Annex was standing at the top of the stairs, a hefty blaster in each hand as the chains throbbed against his chest. He tossed the blasters to one side and burst out laughing as he looked down at her. 'Has to be a joke, right?'

Kira stood firm as she discreetly flicked a switch on the side of the tomahawk and began charging it up.

Annex chortled and then strolled down. 'Expected a challenge. Where're the fifty or so rebellion members for me to battle?'

'Just me I'm afraid,' Kira said as Annex stepped onto the mangled door and then off again, making it rock.

'Feel insulted, you know?' Annex stopped and looked at the tomahawk. 'Really think that's going to do any damage? Not heard about my soul? You can't have forgotten how it tore that skelm to shreds.'

Kira calmly raised the gun to aim at his chest.

Annex stopped and held out his arms, exposing his chest and the glowing green chains. 'Knock yourself out, human.'

With a sly smile, Kira pulled the trigger.

Annex cried out as the blast knocked him off his feet and sent him sprawling backwards, landing uncomfortably at the bottom of the stairs. He immediately put a hand to his chest, relieved to feel no wounding. He was about to laugh when he saw the chains lying on the floor in front of him and looked up at Kira in shock. But before he could do anything, there was an ear-splitting cry and his soul rose up behind him, aware that it was now free. Unsure of what to do, it immediately screeched towards Kira, eyes blazing with fury.

Kira stood firm and stared right back at it.

The soul stopped as if it had hit an invisible wall and screamed at Kira in confusion.

Very gently, Kira raised a hand and ran her fingers tenderly through the side of its face, immediately noticing a glimmer of white in its eyes.

She whispered softly. *'You're free...'*

It continued to stare at her until her words sank in and then it turned around to look at Annex, still lying by the stairs watching the two of them.

The fury in its cry as it raced at Annex sent shivers down Kira's back and, as much as she wanted to watch, she couldn't; the sounds were enough.

And then there was peace.

Kira braved vision to see that the soul had vanished and Annex now lay, fighting for breath, one hand covering a lethal wound in his chest. The many other wounds and slashes on his body were left untended.

Kira laid the tomahawk on the ground and slowly walked over, stopping by his feet.

He looked up at her through one eye. Judging by the wounding to the other side of his face, he clearly didn't have any choice.

'...Don't know how you did it,' he spluttered, spraying blood over his chest. 'Lazis is beneath the main console.'

She said nothing; she just began making her way up the stairs. Suddenly, he grabbed her ankle She turned to see what he wanted.

'Dylore knows where the Independence is...better be quick, human.'

Kira shook her ankle free. 'Where is it?'

Annex grimaced in pain and clutched at his chest. 'Be fun not to say...'

She crouched down on the bottom step to talk to him. 'Dylore also knew we were coming to attack you,' she lied. 'Did he offer to send any reinforcements?'

'Not surprised...' Annex looked up at her, clearly now in great pain. 'Independence is on Burtonia, human... aaggh!'

Kira left him crying in pain as she made her way up the stairs and began running her fingers over the keypad of the main console then stood back.

Like in the Freedom, the bottom section opened up and the Lazis slid out. She quickly disconnected it from the console. The computers stopped bleeping and began humming discreetly, now forced to run on reserve power.

Kira left, pausing only to retrieve the tomahawk.

'Of all the places...' Jake, now free of his garetor costume, paced up and down the aisle in front of Kira. 'How could it have ended up on Burtonia?'

Apart from the pilot and a couple of rebellion members at the far end, the ship was empty. When Jake had heard where the Independence was, he immediately ordered the vast majority of the troops to return to Persiona. Syjet and the once-again-sane Cesar included - minus a few details mind. He knew only too well that a ship full of armed soldiers would not be welcome on Burtonia, and they would never be aloud to forget not taking Cesar.

But Kira was barely listening to him. She was focused on the Lazis. She held the box in her lap almost as if it were a child and sat still, hypnotised by the swirling, electric-blue mass. It wasn't just the colours and innocence of it; it was the fact that her very own father had created this with the intent to save an entire planet. Unable to hold back the tears, she gritted her teeth and rested her forehead on the top of the box sobbing like a child.

Jake suddenly realised what was going and stopped talking. He then sat down next to her and put an arm around her shoulder.

Kira lifted her head and lay back against his chest. 'Look at it.' She opened her hands outwards, gesturing to the box. 'It's so beautiful. Why couldn't anyone see that?'

Jake stroked the back of her head, listening.

'Credits can't buy a planet, so why were they more interested in those than ensuring the survival of their own home? The very home that had seen the first ever human and helped nurture them ever since. Earth was like a mother and they just let it die for greed. I can't get my head around it no matter how hard I try.'

'Unfortunately, it's very easy to explain.' Jake gently kissed the top of her head. 'The people with credits decide what happens and the more credits you have, the more powerful you are. Unfortunately, this,' he rested a hand atop the box with Kira's. 'This wouldn't help to make any credits and neither did the Earth.'

'Credits, credits, credits.' Kira threw up a hand in frustration. 'What was the obsession with credits? Even if I

229

had a gazillion credits tomorrow and became the richest person in Draven, I would still have the same parents, the same friends and the same beliefs. Sure, I could buy a nice new ship and maybe a moon or two for myself but then what? There's only so much you can buy. Even the poorest person on Earth had a soul and credits can't buy those but they're far more powerful than any ship or weapon.' She turned her head to look up at Jake. 'Surely I can't be the first human to think that?'

Jake shook his head. 'You're not, no. Funny thing is it was usually the people with fewer credits that would think like that and write beautiful songs and stories about it to try and get people to listen. Of course, the people with credits said they were just jealous, and the remaining people envied the freedom and carefree lives of those with all the credits.'

'The people with all the credits should have been forced to live on the moon, just to see how lucky they were.' Kira sighed, focusing back on the box.

'Don't worry; we won't make the same mistake next time.' Jake said, patting the box.

'Next time?' Kira asked.

'The Independence holds billions of embryos, including "homo-sapiens."' Jake said. 'Scientist on Earth had spent years collecting them for research purposes. There is an embryo on the Independence for every single creature that existed on the earth at the time of its destruction. When the Lazis is placed inside the Independence it will start fertilisation and incubation. How? I couldn't begin to tell you, but out of the three ships, the Independence is the most important. With that ship alone, you can create a brand new Earth. All you need is a sizable planet with a good atmosphere, which is what I intend to find once I retrieve the ship.'

'So you could start all over again and this time, perhaps without any credits at all.' Kira felt a shiver in her spine at the thought of having that much power over an entire planet and every living being on it.

'We, Kira. We. Who better to help me find and start a new Earth than the daughter of the man who tried to save the old one.'

'I...' Kira was almost lost for words at the very thought of it. But then she smiled and reached up to kiss him. 'We need to get to the Independence!'

Burtonia

"If you need to come more than once, why leave again?"

And why would you need to leave? We have some of the finest hotels in Draven. You want the most exquisite luxury and "companionship" that credits can buy? Spend a few seasons in "Eidolon's Roost" We'll take care of you and your libido. Do you find yourself sitting of an evening with nothing to do except read adverts like this one? Then you've never sampled the night-life of Burtonia. In fact, that's a lie, Burtonia has no night life. We don't differentiate between day and night. You can get whatever you want, 27 hours a day.

But don't start thinking that Burtonia caters only for the wealthy, for that couldn't be further from the truth. You walk down the right alley-way and there's nothing you can't find, at a price you can afford.

Ever tried procreation in anti-gravity? No? Then you need to swing by The Eclipse. And during the next two seasons, all drinks are free so remember to keep your mouth open.

But the biggest development is our new night-club. The Independence. Originally a ship, believed to have originated from Earth (don't worry, we checked it for humans), this ship was found half buried in the mountains on the other side of the planet (still works too!). Rescued and resuscitated, it is now shaping up to be one of the finest night-clubs in the galaxy. Grand opening is in just four days time, or five if you're reading this yesterday, and it's to be opened by the leader of the Centuria himself, Dylore. Yes, we found it hard to understand his interest in this, but if the Centuria approve, we can't be all bad, right? We'll just keep quiet about the whole incident with the three preachers, the ten hookers and a season's supply of intoxicating-pills. We're sure those stains will come out in time.

Why are you still reading this? Don't you have a flight to book?

See you soon, from everyone at Burtonia.

232

True to its reputation, Burtonia's main square was heaving. A mass of species. A third was here to experience what they weren't allowed to on any civilised planet. Another third were just here to kick back, have fun and get highly intoxicated, while the final third didn't want to be seen. They had come, like the others, to enjoy themselves, but their idea of enjoyment was far derived from anyone else's. What they needed was not only disallowed on every other known planet but was even looked down upon by most Burtonian residents. Fortunately, one of Burtonia's many mottos was, "See a need, fill a need". Only today, with the high presence of the Centuria, that third had buried themselves deep in the hadows.

Kira and "Ryott" tried hard to squeeze their way through the crowds; it proved to be impossible. They could see the huge sphere that was the Independence up ahead and the stage in front of it with two armoured Centurian guards keeping an eye on the crowds. Guards were also dispersed at random throughout the crowd.

All of a sudden the crowd cheered as Dylore appeared upon the stage and waved to them all. Not that he had any fans on the planet, but most people were so intoxicated that he could have stood there biting his fingernails and he still would have received rapturous applause.

'Having a good time?' His voice echoed around the huge square as he was answered by a crowd that currently knew no other type of time.

Kira looked at the mass of species around them and then at the Independence before finally nudging Jake. 'Got any plans?'

Jake nodded. 'Just one.' He turned to Kira as Dylore once again addressed the crowd, making them cheer.

'On my mark, make for the ship and don't look back!'

She looked at him quizzically and then noticed a blaster in his hand. 'Planning on making a mess?'

He smiled to himself. 'Going to live up to my name...'

Before she could answer, Jake pulled the trigger and a loud blast of red plasma shot skyward, immediately diverting everybody's attention to him.

Kira ran.

'You're a liar, Dylore!'

Suddenly, in the eyes of everyone else in the square, the party had just become twice as interesting, as the name "Ryott" was whispered throughout the crowd.

'Seize him!' Dylore ordered his soldiers, but before they could act, Jake threw up his other hand and released a shower of intoxicating pills over the crowd.

The ensuing chaos was immense. Species, everywhere, made a grab for the pills only to swallow them straight down and become twice as intoxicated as most already were. The Centuria found it impossible to get through the crowds and turned to their leader for advice only to find he was no longer on the stage.

Kira had seen him run into the ship and was close behind. She ducked and rolled beneath two Centurian soldiers before they could grab her, vaulted the shoulders of a short, blue scaly being and reached the ship. The door was to her left and closing automatically. With seconds to spare, she dove through it and landed uncomfortably on the tiled floor, sliding to a halt beside some pipes. The door eased closed behind her and she stood up.

There was no question that she was in the key chamber of the club. An oval shaped room that stretched wide around her and reached to the very top of the ship, just beyond her sight. The walls were covered in gaudy lights and designs while the centre stage was already set up with the latest musical equipment accompanied by a mass of immense speakers. It wasn't until she looked past the lights that she noticed writing on the blue, frosted-glass walls. She walked over and placed her hand against it to find it cold, and then read the writing:

"Female Tsetse Fly".

The writing was on a small concave section and she pushed it in with her finger. The small section opened outwards and a slab protruded with a tiny sphere resting on it, inside of which was a strange golden liquid. Kira quickly realised that these must be the enzymes Jake had mentioned.

She pushed it back in and looked at the one next to it:

"Red-kneed Tarantula".

Kira then looked up and around, quickly estimating that there must be literally millions, all creatures that had once inhabited Earth. As she gazed around, her attention was quickly diverted to two sections that had been previously opened and were now left ajar with the sphere's removed.

"Human Male".

"Human Female".

Kira took a deep breath and felt her hands clench into fists.

'Kira?' Dylore's voice came over the speaker systems. 'I know you're there. Better hold onto something!'

Before she could shout back, the entire ship began to tremble as the engines were started. One of the huge speakers in the centre fell over with a crash and Kira pinned herself back against the wall, looking for an exit. The only way out was via a ladder and a high door across the chamber from her.

As the ship began to gain power and life was once again breathed into the long dormant engines, the glass spheres began to chatter collectively in their sections creating a bizarre high pitch noise that made Kira's teeth ache.

Kira made her way across the chamber as best she could.

The ship was now beginning to break free from the earth, causing people in the square outside to run screaming, while the musical equipment in the centre of the chamber collapsed to the floor with a hefty crash.

Kira grabbed for the ladder with one hand as the ship lurched slightly to the right, making her lose her footing and jar her chin on a lower rung. Still, she didn't hesitate. She tested her jaw and then, satisfied, began climbing up the rungs.

By the time she reached the main control room, the ship was already airborne and climbing steadily.

In comparison to the ships she had seen, the control room was very primitive and she wondered how it managed to stay in the air, let alone fly across galaxies. However, the fact that it did, only further heightened her opinion of humans.

'It's been a while, Kira. How are you?' Dylore stood in the centre of the room adorned in his white robes, a small blue pouch slung around his waist, the contents of which were both small and spherical.

He leaned against one of the computers and examined a glass sphere before tossing it in the air and catching it.

'Have you ever heard of Bottlenose Dolphins?' he asked, showing her the globe.

'No…' Kira stared at him warily.

'Me neither…' He suddenly slung the globe at the wall where it smashed, spraying the nearby console with enzyme. 'And now, neither will anybody else.'

Kira aimed her blaster at him, only for him to hold the pouch up in line with the barrel.

'Go ahead, try it.'

Kira released the blaster and it fell to the floor.

Dylore gave her a smug look and was about to comment when she grimaced and then leapt at him, sending them both tumbling over the computers as the pouch slid across the floor away from them.

Kira got astride Dylore and rammed her fist into his face, making him choke and spray blood. She was about to hit him again when he grabbed her neck and squeezed, forcing her instead to defend herself and claw at his hand as he reached for her blaster with his other. Kira saw what he was doing and rolled backwards off of him, releasing herself. He crawled on his stomach, reaching for the gun only for an enraged Kira to leap on his back, grab a handful of his hair and then smack his face into the floor. Stunned, he had no option but to let her crawl over him and grab the blaster then stand up and point it down at his head.

He rolled over onto his back, spat out some more blood and then raised his arms in surrender as he looked up at her. 'Do you really think you can win, Kira?'

Kira flicked a switch on the blaster with her thumb and it began charging.

'So what if you kill me Kira? It won't make any difference. The Centuria will still be the most powerful force in Draven and will seek to avenge me. You'll never get to see Earth reborn.'

At this, Kira smiled and almost laughed. 'You're forgetting something, Dylore. If you die, leadership of the Centuria will pass to your next of kin, and considering you've only killed one of your children, that means Syjet will take over.'

The look on Dylore's face was one of unbridled annoyance and if possible he would have kicked himself for not realising it sooner.

Kira nodded as she watched the information sink in. 'That's right, and when it comes to father of the season, you're about as popular as a swarm of migronets in a schneep farm.'

'Then I'll just have to change the rules.'

Without warning, Dylore swung his leg up and kicked Kira in the side making her stumble and pull the trigger, blasting one of the computer screens and setting off a klaxon.

By the time she had gone to investigate, Dylore had retrieved the pouch and snuck up behind her, grabbing a handful of her hair in one hand and the wrist of the hand that held the blaster in the other.

'You have two choices, human.' He kicked at a lever to their left and an electronic voice confirmed that the escape pod was ready for launch. 'You can either stop me or save the ship, because from this height, there's going to be a horrible mess.'

He let her go and ran for a door in the corner of the control room. Kira aimed the blaster at his fleeing form but the ship was shaking too much for her to get a clear shot, and the last thing she wanted was to cause any further damage.

With a brief wave, the door shut behind him and the pod ejected.

'Koontz!' Kira turned back to the console and thumped it in frustration.

The computer was going crazy. Instructions and data poured down the screen in a torrent as lights flashed and alarms sounded.

But the ship was a relic, far older than Kira and subsequently she had no idea what to do. She didn't dare press any buttons for fear of making the situation worse but if she didn't do something, all those enzymes and the hope of a new home would be destroyed.

'Move aside!'

Kira was pushed aside by a human girl. The girl began pressing buttons and assessing the data, all the while keeping Kira in her sights.

She was human but her skin was far paler and her hair was a beautiful blonde - if somewhat grubby right now. Kira knew instantly that this was Domino. The girl that was looking for Jake and who had killed her parents. The girl that was right now, slowing the descent of the ship and managing to gain control of it. The girl that was saving both Kira's life and the future of humanity.

It wasn't the most comfortable of landings and a nearby building lost its outside wall, but the ship landed safely.

Kira was about to speak when suddenly Domino turned on her, grabbed her round the throat and pushed her up against the control panel, inadvertently pushing buttons as she did.

'Die.' Domino sneered at her, eyes full of uncontrollable rage.

Kira fought to release the grip but Domino held on tightly.

She felt her head go light and then heard footsteps in the background. Next thing she knew she was on her knees with the barrel of a blaster pressed against the side of her head.

'Release her, Domino.' Jake ordered.

'On whose authority?' Domino asked.

'My name is Captain Jake Walker of the United States Air Force.'

'I answer only to Grant Allen and General Joshua Quinn,' she replied, her finger resting on the trigger.

'They're both dead, as are all the owners of those voices in your head. Each and every one of them is dead. Now, give me the blaster.' Jake held out his hand.

Domino took the blaster away from Kira's head only to point it at Jake's. 'You murdered all the people on the Liberty!'

Jake shook his head. 'It was Annex. I barely escaped. Why do you think I've dressed as a garetor since then? To avoid him.'

Domino looked at him carefully, reading his eyes. Then, she spun the blaster in her hand so the barrel pointed towards herself and handed it to Jake. 'Sir, forgive me, Sir.'

She stood back to one side in a salute as Jake took the blaster and offered his other hand to Kira, pulling her to her feet.

'You okay?' he asked, looking over her neck.

'Yeah.' Kira rubbed her throat. 'I'll live, but Dylore got away with the human enzymes.'

'Damn!' Jake ran a hand through his hair and then looked out of the window pensively

'We could still catch him; we know where he's going.' Kira suggested.

Jake shook his head. 'We won't get anywhere near Ikondive, he'll be expecting us and we'll be shot out of the sky.'

'Sir, permission to speak, Sir.' Domino piped up from the corner.

They both turned to her and Jake shrugged. 'Permission granted.'

'Sir, thank you, Sir.' She strolled over to the console and produced a small clear disk adorned with intricate blue markings from her pocket. She slid it into a slot on the console and ran her fingers over the keyboard.

'I have a feeling the Centuria might be interested in this…'

In one of the large prayer rooms aboard the *Sagittarius*, eleven high priests, all dressed in white gowns, sat and stood in silence. The only sound came from a radio broadcast, emitting from the speakers once used to play sounds of chanting and relaxation.

'*…Spawne was an unfortunate but necessary sacrifice…I'm going to have all the souls I could ever want…then I'll just have to change the rules…*'

Each and every being present knew the voice and it saddened them to see someone, who they all held in such high regard be seduced by insanity.

'I can only deduce that we don't know the pressure Dylore's been under.' One offered, switching off the broadcast.

Another agreed. 'We should see it as a valuable lesson. Never will we allow anyone such power again.'

'Brothers,' a much older priest rose from his chair in the corner. 'Dylore may have been a great inspiration to us all here and a father to many in Draven, but he also created a strong justice system, of which not even he is exempt.'

They all agreed in silence and bowed their heads as the radio announced Dylore's imminent return.

A few days later, Kira, Cesar and Jake arrived on Ikondive, having been summoned by Syjet, the new leader of the Centuria. They were welcomed as guests and taken to see Syjet upon arrival.

Already changes were in place. The white robes were gone, replaced by normal everyday clothing and many young priests were now painting lavish murals and pictures on the once-white walls.

Syjet showed them to the Spawne Memorial Dome. It was still under construction, but once complete, it would be an immense transparent dome. According to Syjet, whatever the weather, it would be a wonderful place to relax and converse. All would be welcome and in time, she promised that the Centuria would work with the Draven Galaxy, not above it.

On one of the vast plateaus to their left, they could see a group of soldiers, now dressed in their newly designed charcoal-coloured uniforms and training hard. Leading them was a familiar human face with long blonde hair, who offered a brief wave and a smile before running off down the other side of the plateau and out of sight with the new recruits in tow.

Jake was then handed the two human enzyme spheres personally by Syjet, while Kira was taken to see Dylore.

Stripped of his once beautiful white robes, down to rags and with a shaved head, he no longer looked like the leader of a great super-power. He looked like a criminal awaiting justice.

'Kira.' He stood slowly and walked over to the bars, resting his elbows on them and looking through the gap at her. 'Come to say goodbye?'

Kira nodded. 'We've got the enzymes back and the Independence is nearly ready.'

'I'll see you again some day, Kira.' He sneered at her.

Kira stood back against the wall and smiled smugly. 'Unlikely, you're going straight to Hanaan.'

'Ha!' Dylore thumped the bars making them rattle. 'There is no Hanaan, I made it all up. I became the most powerful being in the galaxy just from a little story. Fear, Kira. Fear is *such* an amazing motivator.'

Kira remained calm. 'Yes, you had all the power imaginable, and now look at you: behind bars, finery gone. No one will miss you when you're gone, you made sure of that. And as for the Centuria, Syjet is redesigning it as we speak. Soon there will be no trace of you at all. You'll cease to exist.'

Dylore sat back down on the ledge that doubled as a bed. 'If I created Hanaan in my own mind, I don't see that I have anything to be afraid of.'

Kira shrugged. 'That's as maybe, but you're still going to be shot into a black-hole and nobody knows what happens in those. Hey, think about it for a second: even if you do survive and there's something on the other side, who are you going to meet?'

Dylore watched her intrigued, awaiting the answer but deep down already knowing it.

'Yeah, that's right, all the criminals and murderers you ordered in there. What goes around, comes around, Dylore.'

Dylore glared in hatred at her.

Kira smiled innocently. 'Don't look at me; it's something Jake told me…I haven't quite figured it out yet. But, I think it fits here. Farewell, Dylore.'

Once back with Syjet, there were fond hugs and long, teary farewells accompanied by promises of future visits from both sides, once each had finally completed their new home.

Log Entry - 0.1
Entrant - Kira Malcolm

This was Jake's idea. He said I should keep a "diary" of events from here on in. Well, today the Independence has

245

finally launched and we are heading out of Draven Galaxy into the unknown in search of a new home.

Cesar was reluctant to come at first, whining that we were going to be going too far from Burtonia, but we managed to capture a couple of purple Pavouks...he's been quiet ever since. Bless.

I've not known Jake long but I doubt he's been this happy for a long time. He really has taken this to heart and is thoroughly enjoying plotting courses and searching through all the enzymes, smiling every so often. We've bought a few of his friends from the Rebellion with us too but then you can't expect two humans and a pavouk to be able to pilot a ship this size.

Me? Every day is a brand new adventure. I have named the two human enzymes Brander and Mora, two traditional skelm names. Jake's not so keen and wants to call them Adam and Eve: traditional human names apparently. I can see we're going to have to compromise. Every time I go and look at the enzymes I try and picture what each creature looks like. Just last night, Jake tried to describe "snakes" to me and I ended up in fits of laughter trying to imagine a creature with no arms or legs, just a body and a head. Can't wait to start the incubation, but I shall. I shall wait until I find the perfect home. The new Earth.

Titles from Kinglake Publishing Ltd

Crime Fiction

In the Steve Katz series

Hard Man	ISBN 978-0-9550538-2-5
Cold Slab	ISBN 978-0-9550538-3-2
Jail Bait	ISBN 978-0-9550538-4-9
Black Heat	ISBN 978-0-9550538-5-6

Clay   Cal Surtees
ISBN 978-1-907690-02-0

Fiction

The Wings of Eagles Andrew Markby
ISBN 978-0-9550538-1-8

Monsoon   Fran Pickles
ISBN 978-0-9550538-6-3

Marooned   William Keeley
ISBN 978-0-9550538-7-0

Poison   Jennifer Scott
ISBN 978-0-9550538-8-7

Citronella   Ericka Holt
ISBN 978-0-9550538-9-4

Indigo   Marcus Woolcott
ISBN 978-1-907690-01-3

Nonfiction

Swimmers Against the Stream
                     James Buckden
ISBN 978-1-907690-00-6

Personal Learning   George Tabard
ISBN 978-1-907690-03-7

Kinglake Publishing Ltd

We are willing to consider most types of book, fiction or non fiction. We do not publish picture books for small children. For a full list of the genres that we are willing to read, please check our website

It is imperative that you follow our submission guidelines. These too can be found on our website.

We prefer e-mail communication and this should be your first choice when approaching us. However, if you do not have access to the internet, we can be contacted in the more traditional ways.

Contacting Kinglake Publishing Ltd.

Web: http://www.kinglakepublishing.co.uk

E-mail   info@kinglakepublishing.co.uk

Tel: 0845-508-6032

Kinglake Publishing Ltd.
Office S4,
Ashgrove House
Elland
Calderdale HX5 9JB
United Kingdom

Lightning Source UK Ltd.
Milton Keynes UK
01 June 2010

154968UK00001B/220/P